# GHOST POSSE™

# #2 ALOHA HAUNTS

Written by K.B. Brege
Illustrated by D. Brege

ISBN 978-09774119-5-5

First Printing Paperback edition – July 2010

Copyediting by Teresa McGee, 22 House Writing Works.

For those who follow their hearts and
dreams…even though it's not as easy as it seems.

# One

## The Curse

It was a quiet night on the island, a warm breeze wafted through the palm trees as dusk was setting in. A few stars glittered in the beautiful pink hued sky.

Maleko pulled his moped into a parking space, turned it off, and removed his helmet. The minute he did, the sound of the beating drums began to pound in his head again.

"BAM, BUM, BAM, BUM, BOOM, BOOM, BOOM!!!" He tried to ignore it as he headed into Island Java, a favorite hang-out for the local college students – but the pounding was more than he could bear.

Inside was a hub of activity, and everyone knew each other. Maleko, who attended the university, greeted people as politely as he could while trying to cover up the pain in his head.

Maleko was Polynesian, slim, and average in height. He had striking features; big jet black eyes, a soul patch kind of goatee, and thick, shiny black hair. He was usually immaculately groomed, but today even his slicked back hair and bandana were disheveled.

"You look awful." said Polina as he walked up to the counter.

"Yeah, maybe an extra shot of espresso in your specialty drink, Funky Monkey, will do me some good." replied Maleko.

"I don't know looks to me like you need some sleep."

"Yeah, sleep would be good, but the problem is…Oh never mind, not your concern." He said as he paid for his coffee.

"No, it's on me…let me get caught up here and I'll be right over." said Polina.

Polina was the island's most popular barista. She was half-Polynesian and half-Irish, attractive, short, and physically fit. She had long black hair that

2

she always pulled back in a ponytail, and sparkling green eyes. Even though she was a bit loud, she was the only person that Maleko had ever told about his heritage. It was something that he didn't want to think about or talk about, and he really didn't. It was like he was under a vicious curse, the same curse that he had heard about when he was young – but he never believed it, until now.

He picked up his coffee drink and headed to a small table in the back corner. He knew he had to talk to someone, someone that he could trust, and that was Polina. This time he needed to share the entire gruesome story – everything he knew anyway.

"So what's up with you?" Polina asked, as she grabbed the nearest chair, and plopped down right next to him.

"Oh man, you scared me!" He said as he looked up startled. He was writing in an old notebook. It was filled with odd sized papers, dried pond fronds with ink marks on them, and brochures from the local museum. The tattered mess was bound together with twine and rubber bands."

"Wow! Is that your study guide? What a mess!" Polina said.

For a moment Maleko debated on just how much he should really tell Polina – but he knew there was nobody else on the island that he could talk to.

"Hey!" Polina snapped her fingers in front of his face trying to get his attention.

"Oh no, this is just a bunch of notes that I've been keeping through the years. I'm trying to figure things out about my ancient ancestors." he said quietly. "What I am going to tell you, might really freak you out, and I know that you have always kept whatever I have told you to yourself…But this time, it's much, much, more major, ya know? I really need to trust you…"

Polina's green eyes grew wide as she stared at him while nodding with a look of fear on her face.

Maleko slowly began, "It all started over 700 years ago when Kauai was ruled by savage tiki warriors. They were evil, and they wanted Kauai to themselves, and no others on their island. The story goes that a new tribe, which had been forced off of their small island by violent storms, came to Kauai in peace, looking for food and shelter."

"Yeah, I've heard some of this before…so what does it have to do with you?" Polina asked impatiently.

Maleko gave her a stern look and continued. "For the first time ever, the King of the island of Kauai – accepted the strangers on his island. He felt it was time to welcome outsiders, in order to farm and grow his lush garden island and population. But once they were welcomed, someone from the arriving tribe, the Hoolakeeko, brutally murdered the King of Kauai.

So, the high priest, the Kahuna of Kauai, sought revenge for his king's death. He unleashed the violent masked tiki warriors on the visiting Hoolakeeko tribe, killing almost every one of them by spilling their blood with spears through their hearts.

But, before the Kahuna started the horrible bloodshed of the newcomers, he made them watch while he sacrificed King Hoolakeeko's daughter, the Princess!"

"Sacrificed her? What do you mean *sacrificed her*? Like KKKHHHHIITTTT?!" Polina asked as she drew her finger across her throat.

"Shhhhh!" Insisted Maleko, as he quickly looked around to make sure that no one had heard, and slowly nodded yes.

"Ooouuuu! Yuk! I always heard stories like this, but it just seemed, well you know…most of the islanders are such peaceful people. So, what does this have to do with you anyway? And why are you looking so awful? Are you sick? Maybe you have the flu…"

"I'm not sick. I cannot stop hearing the pounding of warrior drums in my head! They are coming for me. I am a descendant of the tribe Hoolakeeko! It was my family's Princess that they butchered…*and that's all I know.*"

Maleko paused to take a breath, "Except, that according to the story, which has been passed down for hundreds and hundreds of years…the Kahuna put a curse on our tribe. He said that one day there would be a male descendant on this island, and when the Princess came back to the island, they would seek revenge on us! They would come back, and through savagery and bloodshed, they would take over Kauai again."

"Like, they'd come back? You mean like from the dead or something? Is that what you're saying?" questioned Polina.

Maleko nodded, "They swore that on the day her identical returned, they would come back for her and the descendant as the undead… ghosts, to finally end our legacy!"

"You know Maleko; you just had your 21$^{st}$ birthday last night, so maybe those pounding drums in your head are because you're a little tired." Polina stated, with an odd look on her face.

"Polina, don't you believe me? You of all people, you know about island lore! I am that descendant of the Hoolakeeko tribe! They are coming for me!"

"Lore, that's all it is. Besides if they killed all of your tribe, then how are you even here?" asked Polina as she stood up.

"That's a really good question, and that's what's missing from the whole story. That's exactly what I am trying to figure out, here; in my notes…I've been studying, about our history." Maleko said as he shook the tattered book.

"I have to get back to work, Maleko. The

customers are lining up." She patted him on the back and quickly returned to the counter, while wondering about her friend.

# Two

# The Flight

The team tried to contain their excitement as they boarded the plane, but it was hard.

The success of their London tour coupled with the unbelievable horrifying, yet life saving adventure they just had, kept their adrenaline flowing as much as extreme boarding itself.

Plus the fact, that for the second stop on the tour, they were headed to Pal's hometown. The thought of the beautiful sunny island of Kauai, Hawaii, thrilled them.

They laughed about how difficult it would be not aggravating Ira, especially since they had barely seen him after he was humiliated by the Sisu Soda executives at the last event.

And when they did see him, he would point his finger at them in a menacing way – as if to say that he was going to get them.

This time, Ira even took a different car to the airport, and they were glad he did. As far as they were concerned, mean-spirited Ira could stay far away from them.  He was the worst part of the tour.

Once they had their carry-on bags placed overhead on the plane, they took their seats.

Pal and Terrence sat together, and Ming and Brie were directly across the aisle from them. Donell and Harlo were seated behind Pal and Terrence.

Pal felt Terrence elbow him. When Pal looked up, there was Ira, angrily heading down the aisle toward them.

It was clear that he was now more irritated than ever.

He approached them, stopped, and bent down so that he was almost face to face with Pal and Terrence.

"I'm not done with you little boys." Ira whispered, as he clenched his teeth while his putrid breath blew into their face.

"Oh yes, I will destroy your reputations on this tour! *Ghost Board Posse* indeed! The only thing *ghost* about this tour…" Ira laughed, while standing straight up to glare at Harlo and Donell behind them, "will be that no one will be able to see you morons!  Ha, ha, ha!"

10

The look on his face was wicked, as he quickly turned and tried to smash his way into the aisle where Ming and Brie were sitting.

"Move!" he insisted, glaring at Brie.
Brie sat silently for a second staring back at Ira, she swallowed, and then said, "No."

"I said, MOVE OVER!" Ira demanded.

"And I said, *no*!"

Within seconds the Flight Attendant was at their seats questioning if there was a problem.

Ira knew he had a different seat assignment, and by the look on Brie's face if he didn't want to get kicked off the plane he better move, and fast.

"Oh, I'm so sorry Miss," said Ira in a sickening sweet tone, "I thought this young lady was in my seat."

"May I see your ticket please?" asked the Flight Attendant.

"Certainly," Ira smiled a fake smile as he handed her the ticket, then slyly glared at Brie.

"Sir, your seat is over here."

Ira shrugged and followed the flight attendant to his seat.

Pal and Terrence turned to see Ming and Brie silently cracking up, and gave them the thumbs up.

Nothing made the newly named Ghost Board Posse happier than irritating Ira, and he had brought it all on himself.

As the plane began to taxi down the runway preparing for take-off, it was comforting to know that Ira would be safely tucked away at the back of the plane. And even better, there was a flight attendant keeping an eye on him.

"Hey, I say we put another pink kitty tattoo on his forehead!" laughed Donell.

"Out of tattoos." stated Harlo, "besides that Flight Attendant is probably watching all of us."

"Maybe you guys should just leave him alone." said Brie, "you know he is kind of like a snake, coiling and getting ready for another attack."

"Yeah, she's right." said Ming, again using her fake male voice – which now sounded more convincing than ever. She was proud of her acting skills, and the fact that she was pulling this charade off.

Even though Terrence and Brie knew that she was a girl, she still had to keep her fake cover going with the rest of the team – for now anyway.

At that moment Harlo's laptop beeped.

Pal jumped up excitedly, "Hey, is it him? Is it him? Is it Spirit Speaker?"

The team began to laugh…

"Spirit speaker? What the heck, Dude?" asked Harlo.

"Yeah," laughed Donell, "The name's *Ghost Talker*, man."

"Ghost Talker, Spirit Speaker, whatever I don't care if you call him Peter Paranormal, is it him?"

Harlo quickly clicked on the flashing icon of a ghost on his laptop screen.

"Where's he been, and what's he saying?" asked Terrence, until he suddenly realized that Brie and Ming had been listening to their entire conversation.

Ming knew the whole story, but Brie didn't, and Brie was still Ira's assistant. Plus, Terrence knew that Brie was a little annoyed when they went missing in the middle of the night in London; especially since Brie and Ming had to cover for them.

"It's him! It's him!" said Harlo excitedly.

"It's who?" asked Brie, "Exactly what are you guys talking about?"

The team began to stutter and stammer, and then they all began talking at once. It was obvious that they were struggling to make up an excuse as to who 'Ghost Talker' really was.

They somehow managed to convince Brie that it was just a friend; but by the time they went back to the laptop, Ghost Talker had signed off.

# THREE

## HALF-A-TIKI

Maleko quietly left the coffee shop, fearing that he had either terrorized Polina by telling her his dreadful story, or convinced her that he was nuts.

He began to wonder himself, but somehow he did feel better after talking about it. As he thought about his ancestors and their tragic past, the drums began to pound in his head again. He now realized that there was only one thing to do.

He raced up the twisting, curving road along the beach. The crashing surf seemed to be more violent than he had ever seen it. In the darkening night, the stars that usually glowed brightly seemed hidden by a foreboding sky.

He could feel his heart pounding as he turned off the beach road, and up towards his apartment in the denser part of the garden island.

Kauai was known for its exotic flowers and thick, lush foliage and deep jungles. The beautiful waterfalls, emerald colored mountains and steep cliffs, with picturesque beaches of soft white sand, made it one of a kind. But to Maleko, so did it's ghoulish past. He began to wish that so much of the beautiful island wasn't so remote and dark.

He jumped off of his moped and went inside his small apartment, something felt eerily quiet to him. Then he realized that the pounding drums in his head had stopped.

It was almost as if when he had decided to go forward fearlessly, all became calm.

He walked through the living room, to his bedroom, the hardwood floors squeaking under his feet. He slowly opened his closet door, knelt down, and began digging into the back of the closet, moving shoes, old magazines and sports gear. He reached his hand to the very back corner, and slowly pulled out an old carved wooden box, it was tied up tightly with twine.

He took his pocket knife out and began to cut through it, then slowly pried open the ancient lid.

Inside was musty, old Hawaiian print material wrapped around an object. He carefully lifted the item out of the box and un-wrapped the fabric.

Underneath it was another piece of fabric, only it was even older and yellowed. It had once been white, and was partially covered with crusty, dried black blood stains. He shuddered as he looked at the cloth.

But the real mystery was what the yellowed fabric was stuck on, and why. It was somehow attached to a relic of a broken small, half of a wooden tiki statue. He stared at the mysterious artifact. It had been passed down in his family for centuries. He knew that somehow, someway, he was going to have to find the other half to solve this frightening mystery. The time had come.

He quickly wrapped it back up, and stuck it in his backpack.

He clipped his pocket knife on his belt, grabbed a rope, binoculars, a giant flashlight, extra

17

batteries, keys, a pup tent and his cell phone. He filled his water bottle and threw a couple of snack bars into his backpack. He knew that food wouldn't be a problem; he could live on mangoes, pineapples and coconuts, and other fruit in the lush Kauai valleys.

He quickly headed out the door of his apartment. As he closed and locked the door he hoped that he would be able to come home again.

Maleko jumped on his moped, but instead of heading back toward the beach road he turned the other way.

After about a mile in, the road ended and it was too dense to ride his moped any longer, he parked it and began to head in to the deep, thick jungle on foot.

He knew he had to get as far up into the rainforest and up the volcanic cliffs as he could, to see down into the valleys. He would have to find the tribal village, which would hopefully lead him to the sacrificial site.

All he wanted to do was figure out what happened with the dreadful sacrifice and massacre… before the curse of the tiki warriors began.

# Four

## The Limo

It was evening when the plane touched down in Kauai, Hawaii.

As the team began to de-board, they were completely surprised by the reception waiting for them. Pal's parents had arranged a huge welcoming party at the airport.

People immediately began to wait on them, helping them with their bags, putting the traditional Hawaiian leis on them, and giving them delicious juice in coconut shells.

"Mom! Dad! Steven! Aloha!" Pal yelled as he ran to hug his parents and best friend. "I've missed you so much! This is totally awesome! Wait till you meet the team – you're gonna love these bros!"

Pal quickly introduced everyone. They shook hands and hugged. Except for Ira, who stood in the background with the most annoyed look on his face.

"Oh… and Dad, this is Ira." said Pal graciously, as he motioned for his father to move toward Ira. Ira was about to be rude and not shake Pal's Dad's hand, until he caught a glimpse of two brand new, shiny stretch limousines with chauffeurs waiting directly behind Pal's father.

"Thought we should show some Hawaiian hospitality." said Pal's Dad when he noticed Ira staring at the limos.

"Uhhh…I believe we were supposed to be picked up by our company, Sisu Soda employees…and, uh, we need to get our luggage." stated Ira.

"No worries! While you are on the beautiful island of Kauai consider yourself home. You are my guests. Everything is taken care of. I have arranged everything with your company. I have even arranged to have the event on the grounds of my hotel, where you will be staying."

"Oh yeah, I didn't mention that we have 20 acres of oceanfront." winked Pal.

"I hope that you don't mind, but I thought it would make things easier on you and your team." said Pal's Dad.

"Your h..h..hotel, 20 acres of oceanfront? " stuttered Ira.

20

"That's right!" said Pal laughing, "My Dad owns practically half the island."

It was apparent that Ira's attitude changed instantly when he found out just how wealthy Pal's family was. Ira had a wide grin come over his face, as he immediately began to help everyone put their luggage in the trunk.

When he tried to take Harlo's laptop, Harlo pushed his hand away.

"Put it in the trunk." insisted Ira through his smiling, gritted teeth.

"No way Dude." stated Harlo.

Not wanting to cause a scene, Ira gave Harlo a look, then shrugged his shoulders and quickly moved back over to Pal's Dad. He patted him on the shoulder, as if they were old friends, while beginning to ask questions about his businesses.

The team laughed at how obvious Ira was. But they were happy to have him off their backs. They jumped into the limousines and were quickly whisked away to the hotel.

Pal rode with his family and Ira, while Ming, Brie, Terrence, Donell and Harlo were in the other limo.

Dusk had set in, covering the breathtaking island in a beautiful pinkish-orange glow. The scenery was unbelievable.

Terrence opened the sunroof of the limo and stood up through it to get a better view. He secretly motioned for Ming to join him, and she did while holding onto her hat.

Although, the island's scenery was spectacular, he couldn't take his eyes off of Ming. The wind blew her boyish hat brim away from her face revealing her intense, dark brown eyes. Her thick, shiny back hair blew in the breeze while her perfect skin glowed in the sunset – she looked radiant.

She slyly smiled at Terrence when she realized he was staring at her.

For all of Terrence's rugged, handsomeness and self-assuredness, he suddenly had a lump in his throat. He couldn't help but think about how thrilled he was that he was actually in Hawaii.

The scenery was totally different from anything he had ever seen, especially compared to the dull, harsh, background of where he had come from.

On one side of the island, there were tall mountains with a tropical mist enveloping the top of them, and on the other side, a turquoise blue ocean rolling in and out from the pristine, white sandy beaches.

He thought about his amazing good luck and success, after all that he had been through in his life.

Even more important than all of that, Terrence knew he was falling in love.

# FIVE

## PAL'S HOME

The limousines pulled into a huge circular driveway of a large, elegant hotel. A big turquoise and green fountain in the shape of a dolphin was on one side, surrounded by a garden with hundreds of beautiful flowers in bright yellows, oranges, reds, purples and pinks.

On the other side, directly in front of the hotel, there was a walkway lined with huge palm trees swaying in the breeze. Tall round pillars decorated the long red tiled porch, and dozens of white shuttered doors were open to a massive, stunning tropical lobby.

The team excitedly jumped out of the limo and ran over to Pal.

"Wow! Will you look at this awesome place?" yelled Harlo with excitement.

"This place is sweet! You're rich, Dude!" said Donell to Pal.

"Nahhh…not me…my Dad, can't say that I didn't miss home sweet home though!" smiled Pal.

24

"You never told us." said Brie.

"No, you didn't." smirked Ira, as he brushed past them following Pal's Dad.

"Well, who cares about that? Aloha-welcome!" grinned Pal.

The team went to the trunk to help with their bags, but Pal told them not to worry about it, that they would have the bellmen bring them to their rooms.

Seconds later, news crews and paparazzi pulled up. They immediately began taking their pictures and trying to get interviews before the big event.

The team loved the attention. They happily posed and gave short on-camera interviews, until Ira burst through.

"Uhhh, excuse me, I think it's me that you want to talk to. I'm the Tour Manager." said Ira, as he wedged Terrence and Donell out of the way.

It was clear that the reporters were not too happy, but it gave the team a chance to sneak away.

They were handed their room keys at the front desk, and hurried down the elegant breezy hallways to their rooms.

Once inside they were thrilled to see that Pal's parents had baskets of goodies waiting for them, including gaming systems with the latest games, tons of snacks, and mini refrigerators stocked with Thrash Energy Drinks.

While devouring some snacks, they quickly inspected the rooms. They were happy to find that the two rooms were attached. The only team member who wouldn't be rooming with them was Ming – who had her own room across the hall.

Moments later they left their room and headed to the dining room for dinner. It was getting late and they were starving. As they walked by Ming's room, they knocked and he quickly came out and followed them. They were directed to one of the hotels oversized private dining rooms. The windows opened to a fantastic view of the ocean; as they dined on a delicious buffet of lobster, crab and prime rib.

"Where's our traditional fare, Mom?" Pal asked.

"Oh, didn't your Dad tell you yet?"

Pal shook his head no.

"The Sisu Soda folks told me that…"

"Eh-hem..." Ira cleared his throat interrupting.

"Oh, forgive me, please go ahead..." said Pal's Mom.

Once again Ira began to show his authority and persnickety side. He stood up at the long table and started speaking, "As far as the Hawaiian food goes, I will get to that," he said, "but first things first. As you know, tomorrow is going to be a *very* long day of surfing. It's necessary that you prepare for the 'Challenge Yourself Because You'll be Challenged' surfing segment of this tour. If you recall, that *is* why you're here."

He continued to tell them that they would have a breakfast meeting at 5:00am, a Sisu Soda meeting, photo shoot and then would surf for the day.

"5:00am breakfast meeting! That's awesome." said Donell sarcastically.

"That's not in this itinerary." stated Brie, as she flipped through papers.

"Calm down! If you children – heh-heh-heh…" Ira laughed, looking at Pal's Dad for approval, "would just pull yourselves together. Ya see what I've been dealing with this whole time, Mr. Palamau?"

It was clear by the look on Mr.

Palamau's face, that he was not happy with Ira, as much as Ira was trying to impress him.

"So, what does all of this have to do with our traditional Hawaiian food?" Pal questioned.

"Mr. Golden, if I may?" asked Pal's Mom.

"Oh, why yes, of course, of course, Mrs. Palamau, be my guest…" said Ira reluctantly sitting back down.

Pal's Mom went on to explain that they had chatted with the Sisu Soda execs and had gotten their approval to have a luau. It would be the night before the competition, providing the team practiced all day.

"A luau! Totally cool!" said Harlo.

"Makes the thought of 5:00am sound much sweeter!" said Donell sneering at Ira.

"And then we will have some real Hawaiian food!" smiled Pal.

After dinner they knew that they weren't going to have to worry about Ira. He was busy following Pal's Dad around the grounds. It was obvious Ira was trying to impress him, and the team assumed Ira was hoping to get a job out of it.

But no matter where the two of them went, Pal's Dad made sure that his right-hand man, and Pal's best friend, Steven, was right there with them.

The team went outside to take a look at where they would be surfing. Enormous bleachers were being constructed in front of the ocean – to hold the hundreds of fans that would soon be there for the big event.

Ming and Brie wanted to go for a walk on the beach. It was clear that Terrence wanted to join them, but he had to hang out with the rest of the guys. He knew that they had to keep Ming's secret.

As the team headed back to their rooms, Donell looked around to make sure that no one else was nearby, "Hey, I think that Brie has a thing for Ming." He whispered.

"Thing for Ming!" Pal laughed and then burped loudly.

"Don't be so piggish!" said Harlo, who then belched even louder himself, "No way, Dude, Ming doesn't play for that team, if you know what I mean."

"So you guys think that Ming is…?" asked Terrence.

"No question!" Donell interrupted.

"Who cares who plays on what team?! I just wonder why we can't get a hold of GT. It's been almost impossible to reach him since our wicked experience at Castle Cloo, Cloo, Cloo...Man, I can't even bring myself to say it!" said Harlo.

They nodded in agreement as Pal opened one of their hotel room doors, and just a few feet away Donell opened another.

"Sweet dreams!" Said Pal at the one door, as he began to walk into the room.

"Nighty, night!" laughed Donell at the other door.

Once inside, they all looked at each other from room to room and cracked up.

Harlo sat down with his laptop while trying to reach GT.

"Hey man, let's do some gaming!" said Pal.

"Wait! He's on! Ghost Talker is on!" yelled Harlo excitedly.

# Six

## End of Hoolakeeko Island

"Tie together! No time! Tie together!!!" shouted King Hoolakeeko at the top of his lungs.

He continued to shout directions, while helping his villagers tie the string of boats together that were bashing against the shore.

"No more time! We go now!" he screamed.

Once everyone was inside the boats, they quickly lifted their anchors made of coconut fiber and rocks. The boats immediately began to thrash about as they moved out into the angry ocean.

It began to rain harder, pelting the small island. It was clear that the hurricane wasn't far, and it was going to hit the island with a vengeance by nightfall.

The King knew that this hurricane would finish their tiny island for good. This time he had no other choice, he had to force his people to leave…or die!

It was a terrifying night at sea; everyone was saddened and exhausted from struggling to keep the boats together. It had been a fight not to lose each other as the boats rocked violently in the vicious water. And still, they had lost many people from their tribe.

Late at night, they had escaped the storm, and by dawn they awoke to beautiful blue skies.

Exhausted and seasick in the overcrowded boats, they continued to drift in the unknown waters. There was no sight of their island behind them.

"Look! Island!" yelled one of the villagers, "Island, island!!!"

The King squinted, not sure if there was land ahead, or if they were so worn out that it was just a mirage.

"Row boats! Row!" instructed the King as they all began to paddle furiously.

It was all King Hoolakeeko could do to keep positive for his people. He knew how brutal some of the tribes on other islands were, but they had no choice. They would never be able to return home. This was the last storm that their tiny island could handle.

Now, with his only family, his daughter, the Princess, and his people; along with the few belongings that they could bring, they had to find land. They began to use the last bit of their strength to paddle.

They were heading toward what would hopefully be a welcoming, peaceful land.

# Seven

## Maleko's Decision

It was almost dark now and Maleko had to be careful. As he climbed through some of the overgrown gorges, he knew there were places where the knife-edged cliffs would end with no warning. Some would drop down thousands of feet down to the sea.

He shuddered at the thought of plummeting into the ocean against the rocks - almost 4000 feet straight down.

He decided it was too dangerous to continue. The skies grew darker the farther into the jungle he got, and now the wind had picked up. Besides the heavy mountain mist was thick, and he could barely see where he was going. He decided he would get some sleep, and start again in the morning.

He found a hidden area at the bottom of a Monkey Pod tree where he felt safe. He pitched his small pup tent, and crawled inside, exhausted.

Maleko lay in the tent clicking his flashlight on and off, thinking about how he had been walking for hours, searching for some kind of clue. He was hoping he would come across something that would lead him to the ancient temple and the horrible sight where the grisly battle was fought over 700 years ago.

He was feeling frightened, alone, and lost in the scary jungle. He wondered how he could possibly be related to such a cruel past – especially when he hated any kind of violence.

Maleko wondered if he ever even found the site, would there be any clues? Or, if after hundreds and hundreds of years, the lost half-a-tiki statue still existed.

He clicked his flashlight off, but seconds after he fell asleep, he woke up, scared to death.

Something was scratching the top of his tent, almost like it was trying to tear the tent open! It was terrifying! He held his breath, motionless, stricken with fear.

Through the thin tent canvas, in the dim moonlit night sky, it looked like a boney skeleton hand!

He had to do something! He thought about making a run for it, but knew he would never make it out alive. He also knew in his heart, that this was the battle that he had come for!

# EIGHT

## OOZING BLOOD

Maleko held his breath, and carefully moved toward the tent opening…then as swiftly as he could he jumped out of the tent with his knife in his hand. He fiercely began stabbing toward the skeleton hand!

Within seconds he realized that it wasn't a skeleton hand at all, but a twisted old tree branch that had been hitting the top of his tent in the wind. But in the dark it looked like nasty, boney fingers! Only now, in his explosion of fear, he had put several large holes in the top of his tent!

He dropped down in the brush to catch his breath. Now, he was going to have to get some palm leaves to cover up the holes.  He found some, then quickly cut and tied them to the top of the small tent.

Once inside, it didn't take him long to fall back asleep. But seconds later he awoke again by the horrible drum beat in his head! Only this time it was much louder and fiercer, and it sounded like it was mixed in with garbled native sounds and voices.

He assumed that he was having a nightmare. He covered his ears in a desperate attempt to block out the frightening sounds, but they only grew louder and louder.

Frustrated, he sat up again trying to shake it off…but when he did, he could hear what sounded like footsteps outside his tent.

He wasn't hearing sounds in his head! There were actual natives! He sat as quiet and motionless as possible, not moving a muscle. When it seemed like the sounds were moving away, he gently opened the tent flap, and peered out into the darkness.

He gasped! There, in the pale blue shadows of the moon, he saw the most shocking sight that he had ever seen in his life!

Moving through the night were mutated, half flesh and bone, zombie-like, ghost warriors! The appalling figures looked like the undead with rotting and decaying musculature and tendons! The threatening moving corpses had chunks of flesh hanging off of them, some with exposed brains or missing limbs! They had gaping open holes as they dripped blood, while gliding through the darkness. They were hacking down plants and brush with fiendish looking machete's and spears. One of the half-open, oozing undead pounded a dreadful sounding drum – the same drum that had been pounding in Maleko's head for months! It was clear that they were searching for something.

Now Maleko knew that everything he had been told was true, but the question was, how would he ever find the missing half-a-tiki before these evil, blood thirsty zombies got to it…and to him?!

He knew that he was lucky to have covered his tent with palms, or they would've caught him, and he would've been dead for sure…butchered by the hideous zombies!

There was no sleeping now; he sat in shock, waiting for dawn.

# NINE

## GHOST TALKER IS BACK

"What's he sayin'?" asked Pal as he flopped on the bed letting out a huge fart.

"He's sayin' that you stink!" said Donell.

"Eeeeuuuuu!" They all said while trying to wave the smell away.

"It's called ocean breeze." laughed Pal.

"Shhhhhh!" insisted Harlo.

Terrence and Donell hovered over Harlo at the laptop. Harlo typed as fast as he could, desperately trying to get a response from GT.

Finally, the letters blinked in the open text window, "***Hello friends.***"

"Hello friends? Hello friends?! What is this dude's problem?" Donell insisted,
"Ask him what the hell happened back in London. Ask him why he sent us to that tore-up place anyway."

"No, I can't! I don't want to make him angry – we're lucky that he's back in touch with us!" snapped Harlo.

It wasn't Harlo's nature to snap, he was a quiet, kind, soft spoken boarder who was into technology, and the paranormal. But the pressure of the tour, and this strange internet connection on his laptop, was starting to creep him out.

"Guys, guys, cool it!" insisted Terrence.

"Yeaaaahhhh buddy." smiled Pal, who was now munching on chocolate covered macadamia nuts. "Like you think that you dudes really believe that we are the *Ghost Board Posse*. Ha-ha! You know, like we are gonna do anymore of that totally scary stuff, and keep huntin' ghosts or somethin'…cuz I'll tell ya – my brosephs, in Kauai no way! And I mean *noooo* way! Uh-uh! Way too scary for me …"

"Yeah, sorry..." said Harlo meekly, "Guess I'm still a little wigged out after GT lured me to a place like that, got knocked out by bloody ghosts, and woke up hanging in a torture chamber, and all in a haunted castle in London!"

For a moment they grew serious, realizing that they were lucky to be alive.

But the mood quickly turned to laughter again when they noticed Pal. He was now lying on his side on the bed, while still eating chocolate covered

41

macadamia nuts and rambling. He hadn't stopped giving his thoughts about ghost hunting in Hawaii, and now, he was flipping through a surfing magazine

When Pal realized that they were all laughing at him, he sat up. His eyes widened with fear, "What? What my bros? I'm not kidding you. Not a chance. This is no joke in Hawaii. And you are just *lolo* if you think…"

"Lolo?" questioned Terrence.

"Yeah, lolo – you know *crazy*." Pal continued as he made the crazy sign circling his ear.

"I think you've had way to much sugar." Said Terrence as he went to grab the candy, but stopped when the computer clicked loudly. They immediately turned to see what GT had written.

***"Didn't mean to leave you hanging-no offense, Harlo. Ghost Board Posse-while on the island of Kauai, you must…***

"What?!" questioned Harlo, how the heck does he know what happened back in that castle?

"And how does he know where we are?" asked Terrence.

"What do you mean?" asked Donell, "Didn't you tell him?"

Harlo slowly shook his head "no".

"Whaaat? Kauai?" asked Pal, as he rolled off the bed and wiggled his way in between them to see the screen.

They repeatedly questioned Harlo about having given GT any information, while Harlo showed them the only emails he had sent. As the screen flashed, they stared while the words began to slowly appear…

*… go to the middle of the island, down the first ravine, find the luakini."*

Click. That was it. GT typed one short sentence and signed off, without any other instructions.

"Luakini? Luakini! You would have to be *really* lolo, I mean totally *crazy* to go there." stated Pal seriously.

"Okay, then what is a luakini?" asked Harlo.

"A temple of human sacrifice!" answered Pal.

"Yeah, like I don't know man…I dig being the Ghost Board Posse and all, but we gotta surf all day tomorrow, and then the big luau that Pal's parents have planned for us. We can't miss this stuff because of this crazy computer telling us to go chase…whatever." stated Terrence.

"It is not a crazy computer." insisted Harlo.

"Okay, my bad – your crazy laptop."

"C'mon guys, ya know Terrence is right. I mean that whole thing in London was so weird – we gotta focus on this tour. Ira is after us as it is." agreed Donell.

"Yeah, good my bros are finally coming to their senses! Besides Steven says that there are some really hot, and I mean smokin' hot fair-haired maidens checkin' in to the other hotels! And they are here for us, oh yeah, just to see our surfing, Dudes! And I want to be ready for that!" stated Pal, as he now stood in front of the mirror flexing his muscles, while sucking in his stomach.

"Yeah, to tell you the truth, I'm a little worried about surfin'." said Donell.

"No worries man. If I can skateboard, you can surf!" smiled Pal, clearly relieved that they were getting away from the ghost talk.

They realized how tired they were. While they got ready for bed, they made Harlo give his absolute promise that he would not run off to investigate wherever Ghost Talker was sending them this time.

A few minutes later they could hear some talking outside their room. Pal peeked out to see that Ming and Brie just getting back.

"Oh! A hug! A hug!" whispered Pal peering through the peep hole.

"They're just friends." insisted Terrence, "go to sleep."

He knew that Ming was lucky to get her own room this time, but he definitely missed her.

# TEN

## MASKED WARRIORS

King Hoolakeeko was overjoyed that there really was an island! The villagers rowed as hard as they could, and pretty soon 82, of the 95 small boats, had finally made it to the shore of the lush island. The tribe was thrilled to be on land, as they pulled their boats to shore many collapsed in the sand.

It had been a tough battle fighting the rough seas to keep their women and children safe. Many were still seasick, as they forced themselves to get up.

The King was so happy, he bent down and kissed the ground, while thanking the Gods. The island looked green and beautiful. This would be their new home.

"BAM, BUM, BAM, BUM, BOOM, BOOM, BOOM!!!" the air was at once filled with the sound of pounding drums.

The King immediately ordered the tribe to circle together; they drew their spears while the sound of the drums drew near.

The hot sun was beating on the hungry, exhausted Hoolakeeko tribe. The King knew that they had nothing to offer the island tribe. The riches they had were washed away with their island. His only hope was that maybe a bond could form between the two royal families.

Seconds later, the plants in front of them began to move. Suddenly masked warrior faces appeared through the brush! The Hoolakeeko tribe froze. All around them were warriors; they were everywhere, even scaling the palm trees high above them in effortless snake-like moves.

They drew together, as the ferocious looking tribe moved closer. The women gasped at the alarming painted masks.

The pounding of the drums stopped when a warrior lifted his mask. He put a giant conk shell to his lips and blew loudly. Immediately a group of warriors surrounding the high priest – the Kahuna of the island walked toward them. It was apparent by his massive feathered headdress, necklaces with odd symbols, bone knife, and shrunken head hanging from his waist, that he practiced sorcery. He had a thin, angry face with pursed lips and darting eyes as he looked them over, while his lean body slithered toward them.

He was holding his one hand up in the air as his long curved nails pointed down. When he snapped his fingers, the warriors stopped moving, and bowed their heads.

Now the Kahuna was just a few feet away from them, as he held up a huge knife – like he was going to stab King Hoolakeeko! Instantly the Hoolakeeko tribe drew their spears. The masked island warriors moved closer and within seconds there was a stand off!

"Stop! Drop your weapons! I order you!" yelled a voice. A young unmasked warrior pushed his way through the crowd. He had a handsome face, straight jet black hair and kind eyes. He looked strong and muscular with a commanding presence.

The Hoolakeeko tribe didn't move as they watched silently when more unmasked warriors immediately followed him out of the jungle. They continued to form a straight line behind him, blocking the masked warriors, as he walked up to them.

The Hoolakeeko tribe didn't know if they were welcome or not. Much of the tribe was heavily armed,

48

and by the looks of their masks and weapons, most were not too friendly, nor were they happy to see any newcomers on their island.

"You do not command me!" the Kahuna yelled at the young warrior as he walked up.

"I am the Prince of Kauai! I know my father said *no bloodshed*! You were to bring them to our village!"

"That is what I do!" snarled the Kahuna.

"I do not believe you! I will tell my father!"

"You will do nothing!!!" bellowed the Kahuna.

The Prince ordered his tribe to drop their spears, which they did immediately upon his command. He carefully moved toward King Hoolakeeko with his arms open and extended, signaling peace. He then introduced himself to the King while staring at the Princess.

They told him of the deadly storm that wiped out their island and how the sea had swallowed many of their tribe.

The Prince of Kauai granted them passage as he escorted them to his village, and welcomed them onto his island.

The Kahuna walked behind them, enraged.

49

# Eleven

## Irritable Ira

'Rrrriiinnggg, Rrrriiinnggg, Rrrriiinnggg!!!'
The phones in both hotel rooms were ringing in unison.

"Oh c'mon!" growled Donell as he looked at
the clock which read 5:00am. He groggily picked up
the phone and hung it back up.

He could hear his teammates grumbling too.
There was no way that he wanted to get up at the crack
of dawn to surf! He was feeling tired, and very
homesick. He missed his family, and was happy that he
got a chance to talk with them the night before. Donell
wished that he could see them, like Pal got to see his.

His parents told him that they were really
proud of him, which was a first for his Dad. Donell
was disappointed though, when he heard about his
Dad's hours being cut at the automotive plant in
Detroit.

Luckily, the money Donell had given them
from winning the competition was helping his family
get by. When he talked to his little sister, she told him

that she had been so inspired by his success, that she worked extra hard to get on the honor roll.

Donell was looking forward to seeing them soon; but the last thing he wanted to do was surf. He hadn't spent a lot of time in the water. Coming from a city like Detroit, going to the beach was a rare occasion, and when they did he wasn't fond of the water. He was grateful to have taken swimming lessons in school, but wasn't so sure about surfing in the ocean.

"Ohhhh…" moaned Pal from the other room, "and just who is the dork that's already up and showering?"

"Not me! And goodnight!" yelled Harlo, covering his head with his pillow.

"Well, I'll be, if it isn't my roomy, Terrence! So that's how he stays lookin' so pretty all the time." joked Pal.

"Yeah, he keeps those golden locks of his all shiny and smooth, kinda like my sweet dreads!" Donell joined in.

"Hey! I can hear you idiots!" yelled Terrence as he opened the bathroom door. "Look you girly-men,

51

I got places to be and people to see." he said as he whipped his wet towel at Pal's head.

"Ohhh…disgusting!" said Pal throwing it back at Terrence. "Like who, and where?"

In the adjoining room, Donell and Harlo looked over at each other questioningly. They wondered about Terrence's friendship with Ming. They thought at first, that maybe it was to get close to Brie, but then he never really talked to Brie, so they didn't get it.

"Like food for starters," said Terrence, "I'm going to chow, and then get out there ridin' some of those gnarly waves! Oh yeah, I'll be ready for the big event tomorrow, and sleepyheads, didn't Ira plan a meeting today with the Sisu Soda people?"

"Oh crap!" yelled Harlo.

They had all forgotten about the meeting… so they hurriedly jumped out of bed and got ready to go to breakfast.

As they left the room, Terrence insisted that it would be wrong to leave Ming out. But, when they knocked on the door, Ming didn't answer.

"Hmmm, maybe he's in the shower, or he already left for breakfast," stated Harlo, "and are we ever going to include him in our secret Ghost Board Posse?"

"Well, for starters, there is no *Ghost Board Posse* on this island." Insisted Pal as they walked in to the dining room.

Terrence couldn't help but smile when he saw Ming sitting with Brie. He tried to hide his excitement, and acted like it was about the delicious, huge buffet.

"Looks delicious!" he smiled widely.

"Hey, that's my line!" Grinned Pal, "In all this time, I never saw your skinny self so excited to eat."

While filling their plates, they could look out through the open white shuttered panels to a breathtaking view of the ocean and beach.

The roadies were still setting up the huge display and stage, for the surf showing – which really made them feel like rock stars. There was even a team of people waxing their surfboards and getting everything ready for their day of practicing.

The room was filled with exciting energy and laughter, until Ira strolled in.

"Well, looky, looky here, all the children so bright eyed and bushy tailed." Ira said sarcastically.

Nobody replied, as they watched Steven who had quietly followed Ira into the room and was making a face behind him.

"Hello my Bro!" said Pal.

"I'm not *your* Bro!" retorted Ira.

"Well, who don't know that?" asked Pal, as Steven walked over to Pal.

Pal began to explain how Steven had talked him into entering the contest, but was rudely interrupted by Ira, "Brie, I mean *Cheese*, get me a plate of food and pass out today's itinerary."

It was surprising to see Brie get up and do it. They assumed that she was tired of arguing with him.

As Ira quickly shoveled food into his mouth he began to read his list, "After brefast we head to Hanalei Bay for a meetin wit da execs..." He stated as scrambled eggs disgustingly flew out of his mouth. "Afer that you'll be take to a otdoor photo sht. The oufits and proops ill be waiting there – jus like befo. Get it? Then cm riigh baak heer..." The team looked at each other; completely grossed out, and it was practically impossible to understand him, as he continued to shovel food into his mouth while

54

talking… "end spend the daeey practice til 4:00 for morrows shownin. Get it?"

"Uh…kinda, but that doesn't give us much time to practice surfing." said Donell.

"You gotta problem with that?" snapped Ira as he angrily bit into his toast, "And oh…you better be good, or, oh no! You'll be gone! Hee, hee, hee."

Ira was completely different when Pal's family wasn't around. And he didn't care what Pal's friend, Steven, thought of him – especially since he didn't know that Steven helped run the Palamau Empire.

Ira stood up while shoving his last enormous bite of food into his mouth. He briskly rubbed his entire face with his napkin, threw it to the middle of the table and picked up his briefcase.

"Oh, and don't forget, Pal's richey, rich parents have a luau planned for you tonight at 5:00 sharp! Now, meet me in the lobby in two minutes!" Ira barked, and then left.

# Twelve

# The Temple

When the sun began to rise, Maleko carefully peered outside, and saw nothing but the tropical jungle. He packed up his tent and moved through the thick foliage, following the path of the zombies.

As he made his way through the brush, he was horrified when he looked down. There was a trail of blood on the ground, and blood was smeared on the plants!

Maleko hoped that maybe last night had been a nightmare, but now he knew that everything he saw was real! He shuddered at the thought of such sickening creatures!

He quietly followed the sinister trail of blood, but it began to decrease as the path narrowed to a rocky point. He cautiously scaled the point, only to see that it was a dangerous cliff that led to nowhere. It was thousands of feet down to the rocky ocean. He couldn't figure out where they had gone, and wondered if they just dropped into the ocean below.

He slowly climbed back down and decided to backtrack; to see if he could find out where they had come from.

Maleko followed the trail the other way, but he wasn't paying close enough attention to where he was walking. His foot slipped to the side, and he suddenly began tumbling down into a deep dark ravine!

He tried to catch himself, but as he fell he hit rocks, and bounced off the side of the steep wall, plunging through leaves and tree vines.

BAM! His body hit the bottom with a thud. Stunned, he laid there for a moment, and then slowly tried to sit up. Wiping dirt from his eyes, and spitting sand out of his mouth, he knew he was hurt.

He had twisted his ankle in the fall, and had numerous cuts and bruises...but all of a sudden he realized wherever he was, there were burning torches!

Seconds later Maleko's heart almost stopped; he was terrified! Right before his eyes… "Luakini!" he whispered to himself, "temple for human sacrifice!"

There was the ancient lava and stone altar! He had actually fallen into the giant temple! He shuddered at the thought of what they had actually done there…and as he looked around the bone-chilling place. He noticed three weather beaten, gigantic, wooden tiki statues. Each one had a different ghastly, expression!

The temple was eerie and dismal. Almost the entire place was covered in lava rock. It looked like it had once been half-a-cave, but now hundreds of years later trees and brush had grown over the open side, making it almost completely closed in, including the side he had fallen in from.

His hands felt wet, when he looked down – he could see drops of blood around him!

"*Zombies.*" He thought to himself.

He knew he better move, before they came back. He tried to stand up, but his ankle throbbed. He took his bandana off his head, and tied it tightly around his ankle.

He scooted over to an old fire pit and pulled a giant stick out of it to help him walk. He was in pain, but with the stick he was able to maneuver around.

The scariest part about it was that it looked like there was no way out!

# Thirteen

## Sisu Soda Execs

As the limousine pulled into the curving driveway of the magnificent hotel in Princeville, the team could see that Hanalei Bay was like a scene out of a movie. It was by far one of the most beautiful places that anyone could imagine.

The spectacular half-moon bay sat on the sparkling Pacific Ocean. It was surrounded by a beach of pure white sand, and breathtaking mountains on one side.

Once the limo parked, they were escorted through an impressive glass and marble lobby that overlooked the ocean. They passed striking Hawaiian statues and giant pots of flowers that led to a huge private meeting room.

Ira was his usual arrogant self, trying to annoy them with his snide remarks, but his time the team was ready for him. They sat quietly, not letting him irritate them.

Donell began to twirl his gold Sisu Soda ring toward Ira; immediately the rest of the team did the same. It agitated Ira so much, since he had never gotten one, that he began one of his nasty rants at them.

But it was just in time for the Sisu Soda execs to hear as they walked in to the room. They gave Ira a stern look as he meekly sat down in his seat.

Bellmen had followed them in with carts of boxes. The company execs personally greeted each of the team members. It was great for them to see each other again, especially since the execs were so happy about the way things were going.

They expressed how pleased they were with the showing in London, and told them that it was more than they had ever expected.

They pulled out sheets of statistics, telling them that the numbers of friends on their *Facebook* pages were huge; and the numbers of views of their *You Tube* videos were growing every day. Then they passed out several skateboard magazines, and on every cover was one of them.

"Dude! I *am* famous!" laughed Pal.

"I can't believe it – look at my dreads in motion!" exclaimed Donell.

61

Inside the magazines, the articles thrilled them even more. There were stories about who they were, where they were from, and what they were like. But even more surprising was that in a couple of the magazines there were articles with headlines about the Ghost Board Posse.

"Yep, seems like you and Sisu have developed celebrity status with the name *Ghost Board Posse*, and we like it. We think it works." exclaimed one of the executives.

"We are also happy about how you boys handle yourselves, along with your boarding ability. So, let's keep it up with this surf tour." said the female executive.

The execs began to open the boxes, and passed out their wet suits, sunglasses and other gifts. Everything had Ghost Board Posse logos.

"Wow! Wicked logos!" said Harlo excitedly.

"If you like that, wait till you see your boards; and on that note, we need to wrap up."

They instructed the team that they had hired one of the best surfers in the world to work with them, and he would be waiting at the hotel for them, after their photo shoot.

They also expressed their regret on how tightly everything was scheduled, but since it was the kickoff year, they weren't sure how it would go. It was clear they wanted to keep the meeting brief, and everyone was content, except for Ira.

"Excuse me, as the Tour Manager; I do have a few things to say..." He began...

"Great, Ira. Go for it." said an exec, who clearly loathed him, as they closed their briefcases and walked out the door.

Ira stood dumbfounded, and once they were gone he shook his fist at the door. "Humph! They were in a big executive hurry, weren't they!" he sneered.

"Of course they were; they have *one* thing on their agenda." added Brie.

"Oh really, Cheese, and I guess you know just what that is." Ira stated snottily.

"Yep, actually I do – golf."

"Really? Golf? *Really*? How do you know? Why wasn't I included?" Ira whined as sweat formed on his balding head, while his upper lip twitched. "They must've forgotten to tell me…Well, what are you lookin' at?! Go get ready for your pictures! I'll see you back at the hotel. Yep, Ira is going golfing!"

He scampered away like a lost little animal, zigzagging toward the front desk, while the team shook their heads and laughed.

"Good job Brie, getting us a break from him." stated Terrence happily.

# Fourteen

## The Photo Shoot

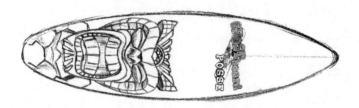

As they left the meeting room, they were greeted by Sisu employee's who took them to hotel rooms to change. Ming flew into one of the bathrooms and locked the door.

"Did I do something?" asked one of the wardrobe assistants.

"Nahhh, she's always like that." smiled Terrence.

Everyone in the room immediately froze. They all stared at him, while Brie glared at him.

"She? Dude, who is *she*?" Asked Harlo.

For Terrence, the silence in the room seemed to last forever, until he casually tried to shrug it off, "She! Ha! Whose *she*? I meant *he*! Of course I meant *he-him-he*! Did I really say *she*? How crazy, I mean, I know – right?"

Luckily they believed him.

When Ming came out of the bathroom with a huge t-shirt on top of the wet suit and a hat on, everyone seemed to stare for a moment.

"Nahhh…no way." said Harlo shaking his head.

They were ushered outside, and taken by golf carts down to the beach.

There was a full photography crew on the set, which was lined with giant inflatable Thrash Energy Drink cans.

Paparazzi had arrived and fans were already gathering behind the roped off area. The same excitement that they had felt before began to build again.

The team waved, and although they really wanted to sign autographs they knew they had to hurry. They had to get back for their practice session, since surfing for some of them was not something they always did.

But as they turned away from their fans, they were even more excited to see five super sweet, new surfboards standing in a row in the sand.

Each one of the surfboards had the totally cool Ghost Board Posse logo on it, and just below the logo was an evil looking tiki statue. They couldn't believe how cool they were!

"Awesome!" yelled Harlo.

Even Brie was excited about how cool the boards were.

Ming smiled quietly, but she couldn't resist putting her board in the sand while standing on it and imitating surfing; even though she knew she looked odd with her t-shirt over her wet suit and hat on.

The photo session went much faster than the studio shoot in London; partly because the photographer had to work quickly in the hot sun. After about 20 poses, he yelled, "That's a wrap!"

They weren't allowed to try out their new boards until they went back and worked with their trainer. The waves at Princeville were just too big to practice on, and the rip tide was strong and dangerous, and growing more and more dangerous by the minute...

# Fifteen

## Danger in the Water

The surf instructor was there waiting for them when they got back. He was one of the best in the world, and known for riding some of the biggest waves in Hawaii and Australia.

His name was Johnny Stone, and had a slight resemblance to Terrence. He had long, sun-streaked wavy blond hair pulled back in a pony tail, sharp features and a strong muscular body. He knew he was cool, and it was apparent that Brie thought so, too. She was doing anything she could to work with him on organizing the team for surfing practice.

The crew brought them their freshly waxed boards and they attached their leashes.

"Okay, my friends, let's see what ya got." said Johnny as he finished slathering sunscreen on his face. "Pal, Ming, you two surf...let's get to the lineup. If I can see ya locked in or in a lay back – I'll be happy."

Pal was the first on his board, as everyone watched the happy, portly Hawaiian paddle out to the

68

waves. He was followed by Ming, who was in contrast to Pal – barely visible.

"Hey, I'm amped, but let's make sure that there aren't any sharks out there, cuz those men in grey suits really scare me!" Pal yelled to Ming as they made their way in to the ocean.

Ming nodded and swallowed hard. The thought of sharks terrified her, and this seemed like a much more wide open area than she had ever surfed before. But the waves began to roll in so quickly, she no longer had time to worry about it. They were turned and laying on their boards. They began to paddle.

"Let's get to the fall line! Here comes our Party Wave!" yelled Pal as they did perfectly timed, precision pop ups and rode the waves like pros. The two of them made it look like it was the easiest thing in the world to do.

"Wow, you're a paniolo!" yelled Johnny to Pal, as Pal rode smoothly onto the sand.

"Mahalo kumu." said Pal shaking off the water, and bowing to Johnny.

"Okay, fill us in here…the only thing we knew that you said was maholo, thank you," stated Donell.

"Oh, sorry, dudes. Johnny called me a cowboy – paniolo, and I thanked *kumu* – teacher." answered Pal.

"You too, you strange little man! Far out!" said Johnny as he slapped Ming on the back so hard it almost knocked her over.

"Okay, great…now that I've got the lingo down I'm really ready to get this over with. C'mon Johnny, let's see how good of a teacher you really are." smirked Donell.

While Johnny worked with Donell, the others practiced their surfing skills. Harlo was terrific, since he had surfed all of his life in Ocean City.

Pal worked with Terrence, who caught on quickly, thanks to his working out.

Pretty soon they all had the harder techniques down and were doing boarding tricks in unison, thanks to Pal's tips and Johnny's top-notch instruction.

Even Donell, with his tall lean body, began to make it look effortless. Ming was surfing like a champion. Although, it did seem odd to the team that he still kept his hat on, and that he didn't seem to mind wearing his t-shirt in the water either.

When Johnny saw Brie getting ready to head back to the hotel, he quickly explained that he was going to observe and wanted them to board at the same time, doing some drills. Then he ran to stop Brie from leaving.

"Okay, before we do a timed run together, can you guys watch Ming and me and make sure that we've got our carving down?" asked Donell.

Everyone agreed, and they dropped on the sandy beach watching Donell and Ming paddle out.

Moments later the sky grew dark and the waves picked up. Donell felt a small tremor in the water.

"Hey Ming, what was that?" he yelled, "Did you feel that? Don't tell me that was an earthquake, or a volcano or something..."

But when he turned to look at Ming, who was now way ahead of him, Donell saw that he was struggling to stay on his board. The waves had picked up fast, in minutes they were twice the size!

Johnny started shouting for them to head in. But when he noticed Ming struggling, he grabbed a board and quickly began to paddle his way out to him.

71

Except the current had become so strong, he was now fighting against the waves.

The team all began running into the water and paddling. They could see that Ming was off his board, and holding on for his life! It almost looked like something was pulling on him!

"I hope it's not a freaking shark!" Donell said, as he paddled as hard and fast as he could to get to Ming! But unexpectedly his hand hit something hard, and he couldn't move his board at all. It was the weirdest thing, it seemed like no matter where he put his hands, he would hit something that felt like coral.

By now the rest of the team were almost to Ming, who was still struggling, while Johnny was screaming, "Get on your board! Get on your board!!!"

Suddenly Donell felt like he was deliberately knocked off of his surfboard! He plummeted into the water, and as he did, he opened his eyes underwater to follow his bubbles up to the surface, but when he did, he was horrified at what he saw!

All around him, dozens of hideous zombie looking skeletons with dangling flesh hanging off of them were gliding past him underwater! And they were walking underwater! As if it was land!  And they were all headed right toward Ming!

# Sixteen

# Island Java

Donell, in shock was gagging, as he had taken in some water and was now gasping for air! He fought to make his way to the surface.

He was grateful that he had a life jacket on as he struggled to keep his head above water. He no longer felt the hard, grotesque figures pushing past him. He shuddered with fear while pulling his board toward him. He finally managed to get on and began paddling as fast as he could while screaming to the team to get out!

He could see that Pal and Harlo had started to head his way.

"NOOOOO! Turn around, help Ming and get out of the water! Turn around!" Donell screamed as loud as he could.

He was paddling ferociously, at an angle toward Ming, and the shore.

As he got closer, he was grateful to see that Johnny and Terrence had finally got Ming back on his board and were making their way to shore.

"Get out of the water!" Donell kept screaming, as he paddled faster.

He wanted to look under the water to see if what he thought he had seen was really there, but he was to terrified! He began to wonder if maybe he had hit his head on the surfboard when he fell in, and was hallucinating or something. But he was so frightened that all he wanted to do was get out of that water – and fast!

He was on his board and within seconds, as the next huge wave rolled in he did a precision pop up and rode it all the way in to shore with perfect balance.

Of course, nobody had seen him master such an amazing trick, and he didn't care. He was just grateful to touch land, as he quickly picked up his board while screaming and running over to the team.

"Don't go back in the water! Don't go back in the water!" he said hoarsely as he dropped on the sand exhausted.

"What are you talking about? Ming's fine, Bro." said Johnny, "Just a rough wave, he couldn't get back on his board."

"Yeah, I'm cool." said Ming who was clearly shaken from the entire event.

"Rough wave, my boney Detroit ass!" insisted Donell. "That was no rough wave! There are some kind of zombie-like fleshy freaks in those waters!"

Everyone turned and stared at Donell, as he continued to yell about zombies, ghosts and skeletons… "With bloody guts hanging out walking in the water, on their way to get Ming."

"Surfboard bump." stated Pal as he looked at Johnny.

Johnny nodded, "Totally. Okay Donell, hang loose. No more surfing for you today. Do you have a headache?"

"No! I don't have a headache!"

"Ming, didn't you feel something pulling you off your board?" insisted Donell.

"Yeah, well, kind of, but it was the rip tide I was caught in." replied Ming, trying to muster up her fake voice as much as she could after such a physical struggle in the water.

"No! No way! That ain't no rip tide, that's a horrifying skeleton tide!"

At that moment, a torrent of rain broke. The skies grew darker and the waves quickly began to double in size.

"Okay, guess that's it for practice at the moment." Said Johnny, "If it clears up we'll get more in, but for now you guys got yourself a free afternoon in Kauai...Except for you Donell, we need to get that bump on your head looked at."

"What? I told you I don't have any bump on my head!"

As Donell continued to argue with Johnny, the rest of the team chatted about the disturbing incident while they gathered up their gear and headed back to the hotel.

# Seventeen

# Evil Feeling

The new tribe followed the Prince and his warriors into the middle of the picturesque island.

The King marveled at the abundance of the fruit trees and flowers, many unique, that he and his villagers had never seen before.

When they finally arrived at the center of the tribe's village, he felt uneasy. This was not what he had been expecting for such a beautiful island.

They walked through the village of huts built from Pili grass and Pandanus leaves. The Kings home was built on a higher rock foundation– which he expected, but it also alerted him, that this King must have many rules that are taboo.

The Kauai villagers stared at them as they walked by, as if they had never seen outsiders before. They continued walking past the village, into a remote area, passing several deep open dirt holes that seemed in-escapable.

Moments later they came upon the tribe's temple. It was a surprise for them to see that the entire temple was lava rock and stone, and it appeared to be carved out of half of a cave. The sides were blackened by burnt vegetation. It had a forbidding ominous feeling to it. There were three enormous carved tiki statues with menacing faces, and two large bonfires burning on each side of the temple.

The King of Kauai was there waiting for them. The masked warriors quickly moved to either side of him, as if to protect him. He was a large, rotund man with a very serious look. He was wearing an elaborate headdress with a huge flowing red and yellow feathered cape.

His son, the Prince, who had led them to him, ordered everyone to stop as he approached the King alone.

Off to the side, the angry Kahuna snapped at two warriors as they began to adorn him with a black feathered cape. Once it was on, he quickly approached the Prince and King.

As King Hoolakeeko turned, he startlingly noticed a massive stone altar – and when he looked closer, it appeared to have dried blood stains hardened on the top and sides of it. He trembled, and tried not to show his fear while secretly motioning to one of his nobleman, to alert his tribe.

After several words with his Kahuna and Prince, which seemed to be an argument, the island King stood up and bowed as he called King Hoolakeeko over to him. Immediately King Hoolakeeko's warriors moved to guard the Princess, when the Prince of the island moved near her, while staring and smiling.

He bowed down in front of her, took her hand and escorted her to the Kings. His father, the King of Kauai, smiled and welcomed them to his island.

King Hoolakeeko breathed a sigh of relief, while the other King immediately signaled a warrior to sound the conk shell.

Within moments they were escorted back to the village as the villagers set out a feast of food. Both tribes ate, while warriors played heavy drums and danced a welcoming dance.

Although he was fearful that the food could be poisoned, he knew his people were starving to death. He also knew that if he refused their welcome; a massive offering of fruits, fish and poi, it would show great disregard for their hospitality, and they would probably be killed for offending them anyway.

King Hoolakeeko also noticed that the island Prince seemed to take an interest in his daughter the Princess. He thought that maybe his request had been answered.

Later that evening they were taken back to the temple for a ceremonious drink, then shown to guest huts, without the slightest idea of what horrors nightfall would bring.

# Eighteen

## Polina and Pal

It had been a couple days since Polina had seen Maleko, and she was beginning to worry. She had tried to call him, and stopped by his apartment many times, but there was no answer. As she cleaned the espresso machine she was lost in thought.

But seconds later, it completely slipped her mind when she heard a familiar sounding voice.

"Aloha Ku'uipo!"

She only knew one charmer who would walk into Island Java, yelling *'Hello Sweetheart'* and that was Freddy 'Pal' Palamau!

"Pal, you're home!" yelled Polina as she turned and ran over to give him a hug.

Pal picked her up, and swung her around.

"Steven, you didn't tell me he was coming home!" stated Polina.

"He wanted to surprise you."

"How are you, Ms. Polina? Great to see you…I want to introduce you to some wickedly cool folk!" said Pal as he pulled Polina over to meet the team.

Everyone was delighted to meet one of Pal's closest friends, and happy to be there, except for Donell, who had to go for an x-ray. They were also thrilled to be safe after such a harrowing experience in the ocean.

They pulled tables together, while many of the locals in the coffee shop would come over and greet Pal.

Polina went to make them Pal's favorite drink.

"Ahhh…the ultimate coffee drink, the Funky Monkey!" stated Pal as he quickly put his straw into the thick whipped cream and took a huge sip. "Mmm… it's the best, my favorite!"

"Yours and Malekos." stated Polina, as she pulled a chair next to Pal.

"Oh yeah! How is Maleko? I'm surprised that he isn't here."

Polina scooted close to Pal and began to quietly tell him about Maleko. While the rest of the team enjoyed their drinks, and got into a deep conversation about what happened that day in the water.

Ming tried to downplay it; while all Terrence could think about was how glad he was that she was safe. He had to watch it, at one point he even grabbed Ming's arm – not thinking.

"Ouch!" yelled Ming, in her regular voice.

Everyone turned to look.

"That smarted." Ming said, as deeply as she could, while pulling up her sleeve and looking at her elbow.

"What the heck? Did I do that?" asked Terrence.

Ming had deep scratch marks.

"No, of course not." She said. "It must've happened in the water."

They stared at the marks, just as Polina finished telling Pal about Maleko.

A look of sheer terror came over Pal's face. He quickly began asking Ming questions about falling off the surfboard.

Pal had surfed that ocean all his life, and had never gotten scratched like that. He knew there was no coral in that area, and that the board couldn't have done it either.

He knew Ming had either been bumped by a shark, or something very, very strange was going on.

He didn't want to alarm the team as he turned and chatted about it quietly with Steven, while Polina brought over some antiseptic from behind the counter.

"Nothing weird that I know of," said Steven to Pal, "just a few nasty storms, but no shark sightings. I'll go check the local channels."

The instant that Steven and Polina left the table, Harlo and Pal's eyes met, as Harlo quickly opened his laptop.

Now, Ming knew that she was about to be included in their ghost antics, and she also knew that she was going to have to act surprised.

She didn't want to alert the team too much, but something did happen in the water. Maybe it was a rip tide, but it didn't feel like it. It felt like it was something that was alive, something angry and fierce…and she knew there was no way a rip tide could scratch her elbow like that. This was something unexplainable.

Pal's quad phone rang moments later. Pal acted relieved as he told the caller where they were. When he hung up, he told everyone that Donell was fine, and the driver was bringing him to the coffee shop.

"I got him!" stated Harlo.

GT was online.

Just then Steven yelled from the counter that there had been heavy rip tide warnings issued the day before.

"Not like this…" said Harlo, as he turned the laptop for the team to read.

***"Go deep into the island…hidden in the dense jungle. The sacrificial temple… the Hoolakeeko tribe, set them free, find the missing half…"***

"Ahhh whatever, no way. I'm not listening to your friend *Ghost Talker* again." insisted Terrence.

"Wait a minute…okay, like this is really creepy, that is the same tribe name that Maleko told Polina about." insisted a stunned Pal.

# Nineteen

## A King is Murdered

King Hoolakeeko quickly woke up when he heard the Kahuna screaming, "Our King! Our King!"

He opened the hut's palm flap and saw warriors beginning to run around crazily, with their masks on! The Kahuna was on his knees outside of the King of Kauai's hut, raising his hands up to the sky. Something was wrong!

King Hoolakeeko began to go outside to see what was going on, and was immediately grabbed by warriors.

The Kahuna was now standing up and screaming and pointing at him! He then began to point toward the hut the Princess was in; while warriors began to pull her out. She was kicking and screaming!

King Hoolakeeko demanded to see the islands King. Seconds later the Prince sadly came out of his father's hut, it was clear that he was distraught.

The Kahuna began yelling at the Prince.

Before long, total chaos had broke out! People from the village were running everywhere. Within minutes the frightened tiki warriors were rounding up the new visitors, and forcing them to the temple.

The Prince was arguing with the Kahuna now, as he watched the Princess being dragged past his father's hut to the temple.

King Hoolakeeko tried to break free to save his daughter, while they dragged him behind her, but it was no use!

The terrifying ordeal continued, like a horrifying nightmare, and moments later it all came to an end.

# Twenty

# The Luau

Drums and Hawaiian music filled the air as the luau began. The team couldn't believe their eyes, as they approached the brightly decorated, outdoor festivities.

Pal's parents didn't hold back, the event was lavish, and they had invited almost everyone they knew on the island.

There were three giant pigs roasting on spits, beautiful island girls were passing out flowers and leis, as hula dancers performed onstage. Even the famous singer Lopaka, who also called himself 'Bob', belted out traditional island tunes.

The buffet was one of the most sumptuous that anyone had ever seen, overflowing with delicious food. Everywhere there were people passing out Sisu Soda gifts and Thrash Energy drinks to the guests.

The stage decoration was unbelievable, with 10 foot duplicates of the Ghost Board Posse surfboards, and huge, blown-up copies of the magazine covers that their faces were on.

The Sisu Soda execs were so impressed by Pal's father; they were negotiating with him to hold tours on his grounds in the future.

"Unbelievable!" said Donell to Pal.

"No kidding, your parents are like totally cool!" said Harlo.

"Yeah, you are one lucky dude!" agreed Terrence.

Terrence himself felt lucky. He was happier than ever, since he had he fallen in love. It was something he had never expected to happen.

Not only that, he even had a chance to privately call his mother, and was surprised to find out how well she was doing. She had found a job at the local dollar store in Barstow, and was going to sign up for some night classes. She was even cleaning out the trailer. She told him how proud of him she was, and that he had inspired her to turn her life around.

Brie, Johnny and Ming walked up to join the group.

"This is something else." said Brie.

"No, you're something else." said Johnny, smiling at Brie.

"Awww!" said the team in unison.

"Aren't you two cute!" teased Pal, "I think I need to go find a fair-haired maiden to fall in love with myself…."

"Oh really?" came a familiar voice from behind.

"Oh sweetie, there you are!" said Pal, as he turned to give Polina a kiss on the cheek. "I meant you!"

The entire group laughed, knowing that Polina and Pal were just good friends. They happily popped open cans of Thrash Energy Drink.

Their laughter grew louder when they saw Ira heading their way! He was wearing a too small, bold colored pink and purple Hawaiian print shirt, and green shorts, that were way too tight. It was what Pal had ordered for him from the local men's clothing store. They got a copy of the room key and snuck it into Ira's room, replacing his other ones. But there was one more surprise they had up their sleeve. Pal had the store's seamstress loosen the shorts threads. As hard as they tried, they couldn't stop laughing.

But since the execs had ordered all of them to wear Hawaiian shirts, Ira had no other choice.

"Well, well boys...I suppose that you think this is very funny!" He snapped. "If I find out that you are behind this in any way, so help me, you will be kicked off of this tour immediately!"

He ordered them to get to the front table with the execs.

The night continued as they stuffed themselves and enjoyed the entertainment. When Lopaca took a break, Pal and Donell snuck off to see if they could get him to pull Ira onstage. They knew that Ira wouldn't want to make too much of a scene, with the execs in the front row watching. Lopaca agreed, and when the show continued after the break, he pointed him out to the hula dancers. Ira, loved the attention from the beautiful girls, and was easily coaxed onstage.

But what Ira didn't know was that he was going to have to hula dance with them.

Ira tried to act like he was into it and began swaying his hips, when the girls had him turnaround and bend over it was funnier than it was meant to be…Ira's pants completely split open!  And even worse than that – he wasn't wearing any underwear under his tight shorts!

The audience roared with laughter, everyone laughed as Ira pulled a decorative flag from the stage, covered up and ran off.

The team wasn't sure what they enjoyed more, the luau, being acknowledged onstage, or Ira's show stopping performance.

"I almost split *my pants* laughing!" said Harlo.

"No kidding!" agreed Donell, "And the sad part about it is, he's so mean, he deserved it."

Terrence laughed quietly. He couldn't take his eyes off of Ming – even in her manly Hawaiian shirt; he still thought she looked beautiful.

When people got up to dance and began moving away from the table, he scribbled a note on a Sisu napkin for her to meet him on the beach.

When nobody was looking, Ming nodded. Terrence excused himself from the table and moments later Ming followed, without anybody noticing.

# Twenty-One

# Ming and Terrence

"Ahhh…relief!" said Ming to herself. She was so relieved to be able to take her hat off, and shake her hair as she strolled along the ocean shore. She was tired of pretending to be a boy, especially since she had no idea that she would fall for someone on the tour, which made it even more difficult.

She didn't know how much longer she and Terrence could keep this secret, without someone finding out.

She didn't see Terrence, so she walked toward some of the big rocks that were grouped together toward the end of the hotel beach. It was far enough away from the luau and the glowing torches that nobody could see her. She sat down and relaxed as she marveled at the mysterious beauty of Kauai. Hundreds of stars twinkled above, and the full moon lit up the night sky.

She was startled out of her thoughts when she heard a strange whistle, and knew that it had to be Terrence.

She whistled back, and moments later she could see Terrence climbing over the rocks toward her.

"Hi!" he said, suddenly at a loss for words.

"Hello." Ming purred, happy to use her real voice for once.

"Wow! I barely know what you really sound like." Stated Terrence bending over as he gently kissed her on the forehead.

"You and me both!" she laughed.

They talked about the tour, and what a job it had been keeping their feelings a secret, not to mention Ming's identity.

"That water looks inviting!" said Ming, not wanting to get into any deeper of a conversation. She jumped up, plopped her hat back on her head, and ran down the rocks toward the water not even thinking about what had happened earlier.

"Hey! Wait for me!" shouted Terrence, "And remember what Pal said about sharks!"

But Ming couldn't hear a word he said, she dove head first into the surf. Terrence pulled off his Hawaiian shirt and followed, calling out to her.

At first when she didn't answer, he thought she was joking around. But when he got to the edge of the water, he began to worry.

Once again the waves grew massive.

"MING!!!" he yelled.

Terrence began to freak out. He moved backward on the beach trying to see her, while shouting her name. He started to head in to the water, when a sudden tremor shook, causing him to lose his balance and fall in.

He stood up, and then felt a strong pull, and in seconds he was underwater! He struggled to get his bearings and stand up, but he felt like he was being pulled out to sea!

Terrence knew he had to get to shore. He was panic stricken worrying about Ming, while trying to save himself! He fought as hard as he could against whatever element kept dragging him down.

He finally managed to crawl onto the beach, but just as he did, he heard Ming screaming for help right behind him. As he turned to look, he was horrified at what he saw! Coming directly toward him were hideous zombie looking skeletons with dangling flesh, and they had Ming! They were carrying her by her arms and legs as she struggled and screamed.

He tried to get up, but the moment he did one of the dreadful creatures ripped some kind of wicked looking tribal mask off of its half-flesh face, with flailing tendons and loose pieces of musculature! It hit Terrence in the head, knocking him out cold!

# Twenty-Two

## GBP Returns

Moments later a wave splashed Terrence in the face. He shook his head, trying to wake up, thinking that he just had a horrible nightmare.

But as he sat up in the sand, he knew it was real! Ming's hat was rolling back and forth in the tide, and Ming was nowhere to be found! He grabbed her hat while frantically calling out her name, but there was no answer.

He began to run as fast as he could back to the luau.

Luckily the team was standing outside near one of the campfires.

"Bro, what in the heck happened to you?" asked Donell.

Terrence stood there, shirtless and dripping wet, with his head bleeding, as he tried to catch his breath.

"Hey, you didn't go swimming alone did you?" asked Pal, "Because it can be…"

"Ju...jus…just listen!" said Terrence trying to catch his breath. "They got her, they got Ming."

"Who's her? And whose got Ming?" questioned Donell.

"Quick, we don't have much time. We have to get on Harlo's laptop!"

"Whaaaa? We can't leave the nice party." whined Pal.

Terrence did something he had never done before, he got right in Pal's face, and stated angrily, "I love Ming! We have to save her!"

"Okay, okay…Crap! I knew it." said Pal, as they began to hurry back to their rooms, "And who in the hell is her?!"

Terrence began to explain that Ming was an actress who was hired to hand out key chains at one of the competitions. But since she could board like a pro, decided to enter the contest as a guy, and won. She needed the money, so she was determined to see if she could pull it off, posing as a guy.

"Yeah, there was definitely something different about that guy – I mean girl, I mean, whatever…So, she's a dark haired maiden, huh?" asked Pal.

Terrence gave Pal a look, not to get any ideas. Once inside their rooms, Harlo immediately turned on his laptop.

Now Ming's strangeness made sense to the team; except for what was happening. They didn't understand why she had run off by herself in the middle of the night.

"Okay, you probably won't believe this…" continued Terrence.

"Wait a minute! I know!" said Donell, his voice filled with fear. "It's what I've been trying to tell you guys all day!"

Harlo's laptop clicked on, and immediately Ghost Talker was there. The team stood frozen as they read the screen…

*"Ghost Board Posse, you will learn to trust me…there is no time to waste in the mistake of Ming's fate…Again, go to the middle of the island, find the luakini."*

Click.

"Why doesn't he tell us more?" insisted Terrence.

"Maybe, that's all he knows." Replied Harlo as he packed up his laptop.

101

Pal insisted it would be too far, and too dangerous. But when he saw the look on Terrence's face, he knew they had to go.

There was no other choice…they were going to have to head into the perilous jungle at night, to save Ming.

Terrence and Donell quickly grabbed their skateboards from the team travel trunk.

"What are you doing?" asked Pal.

"We outskated them last time, we can do it again!" replied Donell.

"Not on Kauai's wicked terrain you can't! But I know something we can do!" stated Pal, "Follow me!"

They grabbed a backpack to fill with some supplies and followed Pal to a storage closet to get rope and flashlights. Then they went out to the surf hut on the shore.

"We need to take our surfboards." stated Pal.

"Surfboards?" They questioned in unison.

"If we can't skateboard, then just how the heck are we going to surf? There's no water." said Donell.

Pal told them that he knew Kauai, and they were just going to have to trust him. They got their boards, and snuck around the back of the hotel to the garage. They strapped their surfboards on, and each hopped on a moped.

They left the hotel through the back entrance, and headed up the beach road, toward the easiest path that led in to the forbidding jungle. They knew it was the same way Maleko had went; when they came to the end of the road and saw his abandoned moped.

# Twenty-Three

## Saving Ming

Maleko had managed to move across the temple, eyeing the giant tiki statues, their faces carved with the most ominous expressions. They were partially covered with moss and vines, making them even more intimidating.

Hours had passed as he made his way around the threatening place hoping to find the missing clue; when the sound of pounding drums began again. But the sound wasn't in his head, it was real!

It was hard for him to move, but he knew he had to hide. Maleko knew there was no other way to escape with his bad ankle, so he hobbled to the other side of the cave. The brush had grown so thick, he was able to crouch down and hide between the rock wall of the cave and the thick vines.

He made it just in time! He heard footsteps and was horror-struck as he peeked through the overgrown brush. The undead warriors, some wearing masks, were marching into the temple!

They seemed to be coming in from the open side, through the heavy jungle.

Now he could get a better look at them; some were missing limbs, others had wide open gaping holes – with some of their insides hanging out. Others were jangly bones! Some of them looked like they had just been unearthed, with dirt and mud caked in pieces of scraggly, long black straw hair, which was poking up every which way out of their decaying skulls! It was all he could do to keep from gagging.

Then it got worse when he saw an even more upsetting site! They were carrying the body of what looked like a skinny young boy in an oversized Hawaiian shirt.

His body was limp as they glided with fiendish smiling faces toward the sacrificial alter. Their boney bodies jolting and jerking as they roughly dropped him on it. Then, with thick vines they tied him to it.

They had captured a human and they were going to kill him!

# Twenty-Four

# Dangerous Climb

"Why are we stopping here?" asked Terrence.

"Oh, you really are a flat lands boy, aren't you?" questioned Pal, who was in a more serious mood than they had ever seen him. He knew that entering this fearsome place at night, especially after what Donell swore he saw, they would be taking their life in their hands.

"What'd ya mean?" asked Terrence.

"This is as far as we can go on a bike, bro. Now it's all steep hiking into vast, mystical Kauai. I hope you mainland boys are ready, cuz this is something like you've never done before."

"Let's do it!" said Donell swallowing.

The climb was harder than they had anticipated. Once they got to the top of the ravine, they stopped for a moment to catch their breath.

The moon was shining through the massive clouds and the mountaintops were surrounded by a thick mist, making it like a glowing fog.

They could only see a few feet into the ravine as they cautiously walked along the treacherous edge following Pal.

"Stop! What is that?" questioned Harlo as he shined his flashlight on the ground along the path.

Glowing in the light was what looked like drops of red paint.

They moved closer to take a look.

"Ouuu…gross. That's blood!" stated Donell. "I can't believe this stuff is happening to us again."

"Yeah, me neither," said Pal, "Harlo, why don't you check your computer?"

Harlo opened his laptop once again, and sure enough, GT popped on…

***"Time is of the essence, to save the girl. The halves must come together; down the ravine is your only hope…"***

"Okay, not exactly sure, again! But let's get down there somehow." said Harlo.

They followed the drops of blood along the path until it ended. Suddenly they could hear the faint sound of drums. Moments later it grew louder.

"We gotta hide, and fast!" yelled Pal. They quickly followed Pal into some solid brush. He motioned to a lower ledge that led into a ravine. They crawled down and sat silently, as the pounding drums grew nearer.

# TWENTY-FIVE

## CAUGHT BY ZOMBIES

They sat as still as they could, barely breathing. It sounded like the drums were really close, but then instantly, the drums stopped.

"Uh-oh." whispered Pal.

"What?" asked Terrence.

"Uhh… don't look now, but I think we've got company…"

They turned their heads and looked up to see the most hideous site! Four shocking undead warriors were standing just above them!

"AGGGGHHHHHHHH!!!" They all screamed.

"Run for your lives!" yelled Pal.

The zombies began attacking! The team jumped to their feet and instantly used the surfboards as shields. The zombies pelted the surfboards with their spears. One stuck in Donell's surfboard, Donell stood up and stared at it. Terrence quickly instructed Donell to help him flip the board over and to hold onto it tightly while he yanked the spear out.

Pal and Harlo were behind the other board dodging the spears. They were on such a small ledge, that there was nowhere to go, and they had to be careful not to fall off!

Terrence managed to pull the spear out of the surfboard, while they continued to dodge more weapons, as they flew past their heads just missing them.

Terrence heaved the spear back. He hit one of the warrior's masks so hard it stuck in the mask, knocking its head right off of its disgusting skeleton body! It sent its skull sailing through the air!

The headless skeleton body froze for a moment. Then began to run around in circles – headless! It got to close to the edge and fell over onto the small ledge, landing right at their feet!

Pal screamed as they began to try to kick the squirming body away.

"Kick it off the ledge!" screamed Donell.

But its ghastly hands grabbed onto Harlo's leg.

"Aggghhh! Get it off of me!" screamed Harlo.

Together they began to beat it with their surfboards, while still trying to defend themselves!

Finally they managed to knock it off the ledge; it fell down into the deep ravine.

But, when they looked up, they were horrified to see that the other three zombies had begun to climb down, and were coming right at them!

"I hoped I would've had time to show you this, but you're just gonna have to trust me!" said Pal, as he quickly moved his surfboard to the edge of the ledge, so that it was half teetering off the edge of the ravine. He then immediately kneeled on it, instructing the others to do the same with their surfboards.

"What'd ya nuts?" yelled Donell, until he looked up and saw that the zombies were just feet away!

They immediately followed Pal's instructions, and within seconds they were screaming at the top of their lungs as they rode the boards straight down the steep lava rock ravine.

They were flying! They had to be going at least 50 miles per hour! It demanded every bit of their focus. It made skateboarding and surfing feel like walking!

Pal would scream out directions to them as they would shift side to side, while avoiding falling off.

Palms and tall grass would hit them in the face, as a trail of lava dust billowed behind them in the dark night.

"Hold on! Were gonna crash!" screamed Pal.

They had reached the bottom of the ravine and tried hard to slow down while averting huge boulders, which they could barely see in the moon lit night.

"Try to stand up!" screamed Pal.

It was almost as if they were riding some of the toughest waves in the world, only it was lava rock! As they leaned back they fought to keep their balance, while slowly standing up.

Once they were all standing, they had enough control to slow the board down, and gradually they all came to a stop!

They fell off the boards exhausted.

"What the heck did we just do?" Terrence asked.

"That, my friends, was lava sledding." said Pal while trying to catch his breath.

"Lava what?" asked Harlo.

"Ancient native Hawaiian sport…like surfing, but instead of water, on lava land …but no time to chat now…we got zombies behind us!"

# Twenty-Six

## A Sacrifice

Maleko continued to watch the most hideous site that he had ever seen in his life. He sat motionless, silent, and terrified, hidden behind the thick brush. The gruesome zombie's lit fires, chanted in ear shattering screechy tones, and sharpened their lethal weapons.

He watched the boy tied up on the altar as it appeared that the zombies were getting ready to sacrifice him… But what Maleko couldn't figure out was why they would want to sacrifice him… *did they mistake the boy for himself?* It was completely different from any of the stories he had heard through the years.

A few moments later the boy on the altar began to stir; then he woke up and started screaming!

"Agggghhhhhh! Agggghhhhhh! Let me go! Untie me! Hellllppppp!" yelled the voice from the altar.

Maleko was shocked! He realized that it wasn't a boy tied to the altar, *it was a girl!*

She struggled to break free!

The zombies moved toward her.

*Oh no! They're going to kill her!* Maleko thought to himself.

He didn't know what to do, four stomach-turning masked tiki warriors, with old feathers attached to them, held the girl down…but then from out of nowhere came the most sickening female zombie! She was moving toward the altar, and she wasn't wearing any mask so her evil half-flesh and bone face was easy to see. She had a few giant decaying teeth; half hanging out of her skeletal mouth, and her long black hair was matted with dead flowers in it. She had parts of a shredded dress on-showing a rotting body underneath, but what made Maleko want to gag were the maggots that were crawling on her rotting arm!

He couldn't bear to look at her anymore, just as he was about to turn away, when the she-zombie got closer to the girl – Maleko saw that she was carrying an ancient blood stained gown!

Maleko squinted to see, and gasped when he realized that the gruesome looking dress was ripped and clearly missing a piece in the front! The same piece that was attached to the tiki statue! The one that

114

had been passed down through his family for hundreds and hundreds of years!

# TWENTY-SEVEN

# FRIGHTENING WEAPONS

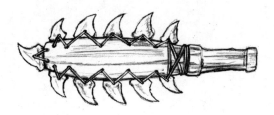

They knew they had to keep moving.  The team quickly picked up their surfboards and ducked behind the heavy boulders.

"Look!" said Harlo.

They were surprised to see small glowing green lights in the distance.

"Someone's over there, look at the lights." said Harlo.

"Candlenuts, they were used by ancient natives." said Pal.

"Listen…Can you hear that?" asked Donell.

"Yeah…drumming." added Harlo.

"Yeah, but that's not like a band drumming – those are tribal drums!" stated Pal.

"It's coming from this way!" said Terrence. "There's something straight ahead."

They moved swiftly and quietly away from the boulders and off the lava rock into long thick grass, until they came to an opening near the lights.

"It looks like some huts!" said Harlo.

As they got closer, they could see that they had come upon an ancient village. They stealthily crept to the back of one of the dilapidated grass huts. Then they quietly and carefully peered through the bottom. Terrence shined his flashlight as they crawled in.

Once inside, they were freaked out when they saw the hut was filled with skulls, bones and ancient weapons. There were spears, slings, javelins, shark toothed and stone topped clubs, and double daggers.

Pal gagged at the site of the bones, "Ouuu, I think I'm gonna puke." He choked.

"No, you're not." said Donell.

"Yes, I am."

"No, you're not!"

"Yes, I am!' said Pal.

"NO, YOU"RE NOT!" the team said in unison.

"Okay, then I'm not!"

117

They gently tiptoed over the bones as they moved toward the weaponry.

Harlo found a place to sit down and pulled out his laptop. He opened it, hoping that they would get some kind of guidance from GT. The minute he opened his laptop an instant message from GT popped up!

*"You must get the half-a-tiki out of the evil one's hands…Save her and put all innocent spirits to rest. Hurry, there isn't much time before all on the island shall perish…GT."*

"Okay, the evil one, guess we have to find him, whoever he is." said Pal.

All of a sudden the drums grew louder. They knew what they had to do. They pulled back the hut flap and cautiously began to move outside.

"Wait! If we are going to save Ming from *who knows what those things are*, then shouldn't we have some of those with us?" asked Terrence as he pointed at the pile of weapons.

They agreed and quickly began to grab some.

"It sure bums me out to think that Hawaiian natives were so vicious at times." stated Pal as he held up a hard wooden club that was lined with razor sharp sharks teeth.

"Yeah, kind of a bummer that mankind hasn't changed in a zillion years." Said Donell picking up a tripping weapon and stone topped club. The mood was somber for a moment, until they noticed Pal. He had stuck about 10 different weapons in his pants and shirt, and was carrying at least 10 more. They couldn't help but laugh.

"What? I want to be prepared!"

"C'mon we gotta get moving and save Ming, before those tore-up things catch up with us!" insisted Terrence.

Once again, they moved the old flap and began to follow the candlenuts, through the overgrown brush toward the pounding drums.

# TWENTY-EIGHT

# THE HORRIFYING TEMPLE

It was hard to see because of all the overgrown brush and vines, but by the light and sounds, it was clear that they were getting closer. They bent down and crept to an opening from a slightly higher ridge, and managed to peek in to where the drumbeat was coming from.

They were shocked to see an ancient tall half-carved out open cave that looked like it was once some sort of temple. The place was lit up with burning torches. They could see three very old, menacing statues standing in a curved line.

When they got closer, they were sickened! The scene in front of them looked like it was out of an old horror movie! Half- dripping flesh and blood, skeleton zombies were everywhere. They were dancing around giant fires and chanting as they pounded on drums.

Above them, standing on elevated lava rock, stood the most evil, revolting looking one of all! He was wearing a tattered old cape, made of black feathers, and a worn out half-feathered helmet. His zombie face was completely disgusting! He had one eye hanging loosely down the middle of his face and half of a bleeding nose. There were spiders crawling in and out of his skull. He had an old broken off spear stuck through his rib cage. Some of his boney fingers were missing and he had some dangling muscle fiber and tendons flailing around that looked like string cheese!

"Yeah, I'd say he's the evil one." whispered Pal.

"Yep, and look at what he's holding." whispered Harlo.

In one disgusting hand he had a large blood stained bone knife, and in his other hand he was holding up some kind of old small, half-a-wooden tiki statue.

Even worse, was that in the middle of this ghoulish scene was Ming! She was tied down on the sacrificial alter. And she had on some kind of old white, dark-stained dress on. They were getting ready to sacrifice Ming!

Terrence gasped, as the rest of the team looked on in total disbelief.

They had no idea what to do. They knew that they had to act fast, and they were going to have to risk their lives to save her. But it didn't matter, the Ghost Board Posse was a team, and they would do anything for each other.

They quickly discussed what would be their best way to charge in. When they had a plan and were just about ready to go – they stopped when they heard someone scream…

"STOP!" yelled a human's voice.

Maleko limped out from where he had been hiding.

"Release that girl!" he yelled as he angrily held up a pocket knife.

Suddenly all of the zombies stopped dancing and chanting. The moment was frozen with silence, until the zombies began to laugh and point at Maleko with his small pocket knife.

"Who the heck is that?" asked Harlo, "and does he really think that pocket knife will do the job?"

"Maleko! A guy I know! I guess so." answered Pal.

The zombies instantly stopped laughing and raised their spears.

Terrence whispered, "Ready? Now's as good a time as any – *let's go!*"

They drew their weapons, lifted their surfboards, jumped up and began running toward Ming while screaming at the top of their lungs!

The zombies were stunned and distracted as they turned away from Maleko, to see the Ghost Board Posse crazily running directly toward them!

# Twenty-Nine

# A Vicious Battle

Maleko kept his eye on the wicked Kahuna who was now moving down off of his stone platform, he turned from the commotion to watch Malekos every move. Maleko knew that he only had a split-second to free the girl. He quickly hobbled toward Ming, his ankle throbbing, while making sure his wrapped up statue was secure in his belt.

Terrence had reached the altar at the same time Maleko did, and they used their knives to cut the vines.

"You okay?" Terrence hurriedly asked Ming.

Ming nodded while helping loosen the vines.

Now Maleko joined the rest of the team to fight off the bloody, rattling creatures.

Pal and Harlo each held sides of their surfboards as they went running toward them knocking them to the ground. Bones were cracking and skulls were flying everywhere! But just as they turned to high-five each other, more zombies headed right for them!

"Heads up!" screamed Donell as he threw the tripping weapon around their feet, which sent them shattering to the ground.

The remaining pieces of the ones that Pal and Harlo had knocked down were now slithering around. Pal and Harlo put their surfboards on top of them and began jumping up and down, crushing them into tiny pieces.

Terrence had finally freed Ming and helped her off of the sacrificial altar, just as the team was getting beaten and backed into a corner.

"Follow me!" said Terrence as he and Ming grabbed torches and joined Pal and Harlo. They lunged at the grisly zombies with the torches trying to keep them away.

Donell was off to the side turning in circles with his board in one hand and a spear in the other, knocking them over.

With the torches, Pal, Harlo, Terrence and Ming were able to move out of the corner.

The Kahuna was now after Maleko with a giant axe. Maleko caught a shark-toothed club that Terrence had tossed him. He went to strike the Kahuna and missed, getting his axe stuck in the sand. The Kahuna quickly backed him up against the altar. Maleko was holding onto the axe in a horrific struggle with the Kahuna!

Harlo saw two hanging vines and motioned to Pal to grab them. As Harlo quickly climbed up, he turned to see Pal struggling with two zombies who were tugging on him!

Harlo swung on the vine toward Pal, trying to knock the zombies off – but he was too late! More zombies had climbed up and they began to twist Pal's arms in two vines, hoisting him up the middle, while pulling on both sides of the vines – they were trying to split Pal in two!

"Heeellllppp!!!" screamed Pal at the top of his lungs.

Terrence looked up and quickly gave his torch to Ming; while she continued swiping at the zombies.

Terrence put the knife he had taken, sideways in his mouth. He then grabbed another vine and swiftly climbed up it, at the same time starting to swing across the temple, trying to get to Harlo.

Terrence and Harlo finally locked arms and swung over to Pal. Harlo held onto the vine Pal was on, while Terrence cut through it. Pal held tightly onto Harlo's vine so that he would be able to climb onto it. Once the vine was cut, Pal, Harlo and Terrence swung to safety.

All the zombies on Pal's vine plummeted to the ground, smashing in pieces – crushing more zombies as they fell! Seconds later broken-off, boney zombie parts were darting around the ground everywhere!

Ming and Donell were continuing to fight down below. It was no use, no matter how they fought and struggled, the zombies just kept coming!

Maleko was still struggling with the evil Kahuna. He had Maleko leaning over backwards against the altar with the axe getting closer to Maleko's throat. Maleko's one hand held the axe as he struggled to reach the statue from the Kahuna with the other hand, while knowing half was still hidden in his belt.

Suddenly a skeleton finger came scampering up toward Maleko on the altar! Maleko immediately grabbed it and stuck it right into the Kahuna's hanging eyeball! The Kahuna went reeling backwards as the half-a-tiki statue went flying in the air and landed in the middle of the sand.

Donell saw it, and began running as fast as he could, while holding his surfboard over his head. Then took a giant leap and pole vaulted himself with the surfboard, landing right on top of statue!

The drums stopped, the fighting stopped! The statue was now in Donell's hands. Donell looked up, and could see Harlo swinging on a vine. Without delay he tossed the statue to Harlo. It looked like Harlo was going to swing past it – but luckily he caught it, and just in time, as Harlo swung to the side of the cave wall. He put his feet up and pushed off the wall, swung back and just when he was directly over Maleko, he tossed the statue down to him.

Maleko caught it, as he pulled his half-a-tiki out of his belt.

"NOOOOOOOOOOO!" screamed the Kahuna.

Maleko held up the two halves of the statues and slammed them together!

# Thirty

# Evil Plan

The moment the two statues collided, there was an ear deafening sound – like a sonic boom! It was so loud and intense you could practically see the sound waves in the air.

The team covered their ears, while each one of the zombies burst into clouds of dust! It would linger for a moment, just floating in waves in the air; then the dust would slowly scatter to the ground.

POOF! POOF! POOF!

Everywhere they looked zombies and zombie parts were exploding into dust.

The team couldn't move from where each of them had been. It was like they were frozen in time! Harlo was still suspended in mid-air on the vine. Donell, Pal, Terrence and Ming were frozen in their spots, and Maleko was motionless holding the statue above his head.

As the gross, bloody zombies continued to burst, they saw the Kahuna, who looked like he was

screaming in slow motion – the entire macabre scene
was silent.

Then, slowly, from his feet up to the top of his
head the Kahuna began to crumble– *as if a disease
were deteriorating his body in slow motion.*

It was obvious that he was screaming; only it
was utter silence – nothing could be heard as he
watched himself dissolve into a pile of rubble.

The minute he was gone, the sound barrier
ended with another loud boom! The team watched
everything spin around for a second, almost like a
tornado, and then mysteriously everything blacked out!

They didn't move. It was pitch black, and there
were no torches or candlenuts.  Even the moon was
hidden behind black clouds.  It was total darkness for
what seemed like hours until …

"Pssst…pssst…hey! My bros, you there?  Cuz,
like, you know – that was just like totally
supernatural!" whispered Pal.

But before anyone could answer him, there
was a slight tremor and another loud BOOM!  The
torches instantly re-lit themselves!

They looked around and realized that they
could move. But to their astonishment, they were all

standing side-by-side against one of the temple walls, holding their surfboards.

There wasn't overgrown brush; no vines, no moss, and no piles of dust. The temple and the three tiki statues no longer looked ancient.

Terrence grabbed Ming's hand and held on tightly. They noticed that her clothes had changed back to normal.

"Hey, where's Maleko?" questioned Donell.

"I'm right here." said Maleko, from behind.

Moments later they heard voices coming. They ducked down, behind their boards. They could see two men in full length feathered capes; one was made of all bright red and yellow feathers with a matching feathered helmet.

Ming immediately gasped when she saw the second man storm into the temple. Terrence gently covered her mouth. It was the evil Kahuna in a shiny black feathered cape, *and he was fully human!*

Before they knew it the warriors began to pound the drums again, while a different looking tribe was being forced into the temple by the masked tiki warriors.

Pal began to poke everyone, trying to get their attention, when he saw someone who looked exactly like Maleko escorting the King!

"It's just like Polina said!  He is the ancestor! He looks just like that dude!" whispered Pal.

"But, I thought that I was a descendant of the Hoolakeeko tribe." Said Maleko

They were even more stunned, when they saw a young woman, who looked exactly like Ming, walking next to another tribe's king, King Hoolakeeko!

The King of Kauai welcomed them with his son, the Prince – Maleko's double!  Together they walked up to the sacred altar – where the Kahuna stood.

The King of Kauai then turned and took an open coconut from a maiden, and placed it on the altar. The place was silent.

Each of the Kings drank from the coconut. But while the new arriving King Hoolakeeko drank, the team watched the Kahuna steal his knife from behind! Then he secretly hid it underneath his own cape! But it was something only the team could see from where they were!

"Welcome to our land! It is time to welcome newcomers! May we all live in peace and abundance." said the King of Kauai.

# THIRTY-ONE

# MALEKO – THE PRINCE

The team watched as everyone was escorted away from the temple except the King of Kauai and the Kahuna.

"Hey that Prince is diggin' Ming's twin!" said Donell.

They continued watching the two at the altar, as their voices grew loud and agitated, and they started to argue.

"I do not want them here! They will ruin our sacred land! We fed them, that is enough!" yelled the Kahuna.

"We must open our hearts and help these people – they are left with nothing." replied the King.

"And they bring nothing! They would be perfect to sacrifice to the gods!" insisted the Kahuna.

"NO! No more sacrifice!" yelled the King as he kneeled down at the altar.

"I am the King! You must trust my judgment. They will stay and be part of our island and…"

"And use all of our resources…"
interrupted the Kahuna.

"Enough! I decide what is best for my
people – not you!" said the King.

The Kahuna quietly withdrew the knife he had
stolen from the other King.

"NO! Watch out!" screamed Ming.

But they couldn't hear her.

"That is fine, my King." said the Kahuna as he
patted the King on the back with one hand, and
jammed the knife into his back with the other!

The team tried, but they couldn't move from
where they were. It was almost as if they were in some
kind of transparent box.

Blood poured from the Kings back as he
slumped over.

The vicious Kahuna smiled and then quickly
left the temple. Moments later he was back,
summoning tiki warriors to take the King's body to his
hut, and to leave the knife in it. They did so
immediately, and the Kahuna followed them.

Within seconds drums began to pound and you
could hear the Kahuna shouting, "Our King! Our
King!"

Suddenly the warriors were dragging the Princess, Ming's double, in to the temple, and right behind her, her father – King Hoolakeeko, was being dragged in too.

The Princess struggled as tribeswomen put a strange, sheer white dress on her, and began tying her to the sacrificial altar! It was the same white dress they had put on Ming – only now it was brand new!

"I demand to know what is happening! Take me to your King!" King Hoolakeeko yelled as the Kahuna entered the temple.

"I now rule this island!" hollered the Kahuna.

"STOP! What are you doing to our new people?" asked the Prince as he came running into the temple. "I told you he was innocent! And you do not rule this island!"

The Kahuna began shouting that they must make a sacrifice, while warriors brought in the murdered King's body.

"That is the knife of the visitors you so welcome, that is the knife of King Hoolakeeko!" The Kahuna yelled.

"Someone took it from me!" screamed King Hoolakeeko.

136

The Prince began to yell in the Kahuna's face.

"Siiiiilennnnnce!" screamed the Kahuna, as he struck the Prince across the face, knocking him to the ground.

"Your Princess will now join *our* departed King!" said the Kahuna.

"No!!! You are lolo!" The King yelled while continuing to struggle in the warriors grasp.

"You took our King!" the Kahuna bellowed.

"You lie! I did nothing!"

"You killed our King, and now we seek revenge!" The Kahuna yelled back as he raised his bone knife up to the sky and began chanting."

"Father! Help me! Help!" cried the Princess.

Loud drums began to bang, as the Kahuna continued to chant.

The masked warriors with dreadful weapons began to dance around the Kahuna.

Frightening women came running into the temple and formed a circle. They had freakish white painted faces and were dressed in shredded gowns made of burnt black fabric and long grass. They would run up and touch the Princess and then run back to their circle. Then they would all bend down and pick

137

up a handful of the black lava sand and pour it over their hearts while swaying to the pounding drums.

The King struggled to break free as he watched the grim scene unfold.

"He will pay with his daughter's life!" bellowed the Kahuna.

The drums grew louder as the Kahuna held the knife high above the Princess while chanting loudly.

He was getting ready to stab the Princess!

The Prince began to wake up. He eyed a small wooden tiki statue near the base of the large statues.

The drums were pounding louder…the Prince reached for the small tiki…the Kahuna was yelling his horrible chant…then, just as the Kahuna began to lower his knife toward the Princess, the Prince threw the statue!

The statue hit the knife as it was lowering, splitting the statue in half! One half of it stuck on the knife, as the knife pinned it to the white dress and cut the Princesses leg.  While the other half of the statue flew backwards, hitting the Kahuna in the face, knocking his eye out! It sent him spinning backward. He was screaming in pain, as his eye dangled and blood ran down his face.

138

The Prince ran and pulled the knife and half-a-tiki from the altar, while freeing the Princess.

The Kahuna staggered to stand up, while yelling, "A curse forever on Princess Hoolakeeko and Prince Maleko when the…"

"Hey! Did I hear him right? Did he just say my name? Did he just say *Prince Maleko*?" Maleko gasped.

The team nodded in bewilderment, as they continued to watch what really happened hundreds of years ago unfold before their very eyes!

The Prince held the half-a-tiki up as he and the Princess backed away! Instantly a massive fight broke out between the two tribes.

The Prince and the Princess managed to get away, and ran into the jungle escaping together. The Kahuna started to go after them, but King Hoolakeeko stepped on his cape, stopping him. A fight to the death of them continued.

# THIRTY-TWO

## SPIRITS FREED

At that exact moment, the sound wave hit again and it was like everything went into *fast forward*! It was so fast that you could no longer see what was happening, everything was just spinning. The team still cowered in a group, using their surfboards to shield them from the blowing dirt and sand. Then, just as fast as it began, it stopped!

They slowly lifted their heads and stood up to see that the temple was ancient again. They were hidden in thick overgrown foliage! It was exactly as it was when they first discovered it…only there were no torches or warriors, no candlenuts, no Kahuna…and no zombies! The giant tiki statues were again, faded and weathered, covered with moss and vines. The temple had turned back to present time!

Suddenly, they heard coughing.

"Look! It's Maleko!" yelled Donell pointing to the other side of the temple.

They dropped their surfboards and ran over to Maleko who was now laying face down, while trying to sit up.

They hurried over to help him. Maleko was holding the tiki statue in his hand, and it was in one piece! There was no bloody fabric, and not even a sign that it had ever been split in two.

*Click, Click, Hmmmm...*

Harlo quickly opened his laptop. "Ghost Talker is on!"

They all moved next to Harlo as he read...

*"You've seen for your own eyes, the horrible fate one evil, greedy man brought upon peaceful people coming together on the small island of Kauai. After the Prince saved the Princess, they escaped far away to another part of the island...but the Kahuna had already put a curse on them. So it was, when the fighting between the two tribes broke out, but a few villagers and warriors remained alive, to heal their wounds and live in peace. The Prince and Princess returned and married. And so you Ming, who were so identical in face to Princess Hoolakeeko, with the timing of your arrival on this island, along with Maleko –a descendant of not just the Kauai tribe, but*

*the Hoolakeeko tribe combined, had to break the evil curse, which the undead followed. And now, that the truth of the wicked Kahuna has come to light...the spirits can rest. Thanks to you they are set free. GT."*

The laptop screen went black.

"You okay, dude?" Pal asked Maleko.

"Just a sore ankle, but glad we're alive." nodded Maleko.

"What about you, uh...Princess Ming?" asked Donell.

"Yeah, I'm okay..."replied Ming in her own voice, "But I'm really ready to get out of here." She added in her impostor male voice.

They laughed and smiled at her. They now knew that she certainly belonged as a member of the Ghost Board Posse.

Maleko looked at the tiki, which he would take to the museum. He went and picked up his backpack and pulled his book of notes out, then placed it on the ravaged altar.

"What's that?" asked Harlo.

"A mystery explained. What about that message?" asked Maleko.

"Same thing…a mystery explained." smiled Harlo.

"We better get back." said Terrence as he pulled Ming next to him.

# Thirty-Three

# To the Hotel

They dug out their flashlights and began making their way back out of the temple ruins. There was no sense in dragging their surfboards with them. They were ruined beyond repair.

It was a big climb and a long walk, as they helped Maleko.

Dawn began to break by the time they got out of the jungle, and back to the mopeds.

They said their good-byes to Maleko and told him they would see him at the competition.

Now they had to hurry – if they didn't make it back to the hotel before the morning, and Ira found them missing the tour would be over!

Pal knew another way around the back of the hotel. They pulled the mopeds onto the long winding driveway that led into the back. He also had a master key to get them in through the employee's entrance.

Once inside they ducked down in the hallways, and quietly crept to their rooms.

Although they couldn't believe the terror that they had just been through, they knew that they had to get a couple of hours of sleep, otherwise the day would be a total disaster.

Terrence walked Ming to her room, but knew that he had to leave quickly – just in case snoopy Ira was anywhere around. He gave her a quick kiss on the cheek, and told her that he was just grateful she was safe. When he went to walk away she pulled him back and gently kissed him on the lips.

"You were telling the truth about what happened to you in London, weren't you?" Ming whispered.

Terrence nodded, "I always tell the truth."

Ming smiled and opened the door to her room, as Terrence walked back to his room.

He was hoping that he wouldn't be teased when he got back. But everyone was already fast asleep. He picked up the phone, as Pal groggily said that he already called the front desk for a wake-up call.

Terrence quietly replaced the phone, even though he was really going to call Ming.

# Thirty-Four

## Ira Fail

It seemed like it had only been about five minutes when there was pounding on their door.

"Go away!" yelled Donell.

"Get up!" stated Brie into the door.

"Whaaaaa…Huh?" stirred Harlo.

"Oh crap! It's BRRRIIIEEE!" said Donell, as he jumped out of bed and threw on his shorts.

He ran and opened the door.

Brie slid in the room and started yelling at them to get up. She told them that Ira was at breakfast waiting for them. They had to go over the event's itinerary, and if they weren't there in 5 minutes, he was going to write them up for unruly behavior.

"Unruly behavior?" yelled Donell, "we were sleeping!"

"Yeah!" Harlo agreed.

"I know, but just get to the dining room – NOW! I told him I was going to the bathroom!" said

Brie as she quickly left the room, and headed down the hall to wake up Ming.

They threw on any clothes that they could find. Some of them dirty from their ghost boarding adventure the night before.

When they entered the dining room, they looked a mess. But they couldn't help but laugh at the site of Ira; all they could remember was him onstage, ripping his pants.

"A little too much luau for you kiddies?" snapped Ira, knowing they were laughing at him. "Seems to me you left the luau a little early to be so tired. I demand to know where you went and what you did!"

The team stopped laughing and slunk into their seats.

Ira was now pacing around them, poking at them from behind, grilling them as to what they did. He told them that he had knocked on their rooms, and they weren't in by curfew.

They kept their heads down while eating their breakfast.

"Uhh…nobody is saying a word? Huh? Huh? Things aren't so funny now, are they? Well maybe this will make you talk?" He said as he held up a small stack of papers. "One for each of you…since you can't tell me where you were – I am writing you up."

They glanced up just in time to see Pal's dad and Steven walking up behind Ira.

"I'll take those!" said Pal's Dad.

He took the papers out of Ira's hand.

"Well thank you, Mr. Palamau, as you can see they do not behave…They…"

Pal's Dad ripped the papers in two.

"They were with me." He stated, glaring at Ira.

"Oh, oh…I see…but…" Ira began.

Pal's Dad told the team he would see them at the event and left the room.

Ira was steaming. His whole face and his balding head had completely turned red. He was madder than ever.

They quietly finished their meal. Ira slapped itineraries down next to them, and then stormed out of the room.

# Thirty-Five

# The Hawaiian Tour

As they hurried back to their rooms to get ready, Pal whispered, "I told Steven to round up some extra boards, that I would explain later... hopefully nobody will notice."

"Ohhh...I don't know about that, dude – how could those execs not see that those new Ghost Board Posse surfboards aren't there?" questioned Donell.

They were filled with a giant mix of emotions, from complete nervousness about the showing, to a feeling of total confidence after solving another paranormal mystery.

They headed to the conference room to meet the security guards who would be escorting them for the day.

Once outside, they were shocked to see the entire area packed with thousands of people. The rows of bleachers were full, and there were long lines of people who were waiting to get in!

The parking lot was packed, as police directed cars to the makeshift parking lots across the street. There were cars lined up for as far as you could see.

Tents were set up in rows with people from Sisu Soda selling Thrash Energy drinks, hats, key chains, programs and t-shirts with the team's logo.

Lining each side of the entryway were enormous white flags with their pictures on them.

Photographers were busy taking pictures of fans with their standees.

There was a Hawaiian band that was playing on a massive stage and hula dancers.

Paparazzi were everywhere, and within seconds of them being noticed – girls started screaming and tons of paparazzi circled them. The whole scene was overwhelming as cameras flashed and reporters pushed to interview them!

"Good thing we made it back." said Terrence, while the team waved to the fans.

Steven pushed through the mob of people, past security and the Sisu Execs.

"The boards are all there – lined up and waxed – ready to go. They've been there all night." He whispered to Pal.

"Really?" Pal asked, confused.

"Yeah, and I had a team snorkeling in the water, but they didn't find anything. What were they looking for again?"

Luckily, Pal didn't have time to answer, as they were ushered to the stage by security.

The band stopped as Pal's Dad and the Sisu Soda executives began to make announcements. When the team was introduced, the crowd went wild! Girls were screaming and people were holding up signs that read, "We love the Ghost Board Posse!"

It was show time…as they made their way off the stage, they were handed their Ghost Board Posse surfboards – that looked brand new! They were shocked, but knew they couldn't say a word with people everywhere.

They took their boards, and headed to the water to thunderous applause, as the MC began making announcements.

Donell moved over to Pal with a horrified look on his face, as Pal said under his breath, "Just feel the love…" He reassured him that Steven had divers in the water all morning checking it out, and nothing was there.

# Thirty-Six

# Perfect Surfing

They quickly focused, as they nodded to each other to make sure that their timing was precise, while walking in to the water.

Harlo tripped on his leash, and then did a quick jump and bow, as massive applause filled the air. They were putting on the show that they were known for, as they began to paddle out.

There was an eerie, calm feeling in the ocean, yet with ideal six-foot breaks.

They got to the perfect spot and into their line-up, and before long a cliff-like wall of water was heading their way. Their skills kicked in on the massive wall of water and they took the drop…it was more perfect than anything they could've dreamed of!

They continued with their unbelievable boarding skills; cross stepping, and doing 180's as they rode in, sometimes in perfect form. It was almost as if the ocean…and something else was guiding their boards over the turquoise glass water.

The showing was a massive success; partly due to the team's determination, partly due to the beautiful sunny day and flawless waves…and partly due to the unknown.

They took their bows.

"I've got one word to describe this…" stated Pal as he waved and did his little dance on the stage to thunderous cheering.

"Oh yeah, what's that?" asked Terrence.

"Epic." He replied.

The team got a standing ovation, and as they did, they lifted Ming – who was now in her full 'male' apparel, up on their shoulders. She was the star of the day, and she deserved some props!

She smiled at Terrence. Ming knew that the rest of the tour would be a lot easier with them knowing that she was a girl, and who she was as a person.

# Thirty-Seven

## Freaky Reporter

After the show, the team happily signed autographs for hours, and then were quickly escorted into the hotel – which was off limits to the public for the day.  They changed into new Ghost Board Posse apparel for the afternoon press conference.

This time there were more reporters than ever. It seemed like they were from all over the globe, and the camera flashes were blinding.

They joked around, answered questions and posed. Until, some weird questions came up from one of the reporters in the back of the room, "Regarding the name *Ghost Board Posse*, can you explain that?"

They gave Harlo a nod to answer.

"Uhhh…No, not really. It's kind of a crazy story and the name just stuck."

But this reporter was persistent and wanted to know about the name, the story, and why they used it, and why the company adapted it so quickly to the international tour.  The team joked with him, by asking him what his name was, but shock showed on their faces when he answered that he just goes by the initials 'GT.'

They immediately stood up trying to see who the reporter was…but the room was too crowded. Pal's dad who had been overseeing the conference could tell that the team was shaken by the reporter's questions, and assumed that they were worn out. He hurriedly spoke with one of the Sisu Soda execs about wrapping it up.

But as he did, Ira interrupted, insisting that it was their job to answer questions from the press.

Luckily, the execs didn't value Ira's opinion, and decided to follow Pal's dad's advice; especially since they all had flights to catch later that night.

Security escorted them back to their rooms. Donell mumbled to Harlo, "That was weird…we gotta see if GT is online…."

Harlo nodded, as did Pal. Terrence and Ming were too busy making eyes at each other. Once inside, Harlo flipped open his laptop. GT instantly flashed online…

*"Good to see you. Nice work with the press…but better work at freeing ancient Hawaiian*

*spirits.  Enjoy your time at home, see you in the snow.”*

And then he clicked off.

“Whaaaa…How the heck does he know that?” squealed Pal.

“This is too scary for me!” agreed Donell.

“Scary for you?  I gotta stay here in Kauai without my Posse!” stated Pal.

“Yeah, ya know, I’m really gonna miss you guys.” said Terrence, patting them on the back.

“*Guys*?  Don’t you mean guys and gal?” joked Harlo.

They started to tease Terrence and Ming. The entire team had become like family, and they knew that it would be hard being away from each other for the next few months.

But, they felt good about going back home; as for each one of them, not only had their lives changed, but they had changed lives from the past.

## Aloha

## The Breges

Author Karen Bell-Brege is a comic and public speaker, as well as the director of an improv comedy troupe. Illustrator Darrin Brege is also a comic and a radio personality. He has created hundreds of illustrations for major corporations, as well as picture books and movie posters.

The Brege family lives in a funky, old townhouse in the Midwest and they love to laugh and have fun! On rainy nights they sit around making up crazy, scary stories.

**The Breges have an outstanding high-energy, fun, edu-tainment presentation for schools, libraries, organizations and associations. If you would like more information email: karen@teambcreative.com.**

**(If you are a student, please have someone from your school contact the Breges.)**

Your interactive presentation was just as amazing as your interactive books-that I cannot keep on my shelves!
*Denise Brandt, Elementary School Media Specialist, Bloomfield, MI.*

It was obvious that their act was a smash by the line of smiling faces waiting for an autograph, picture or book purchase at the end. When looking for an act that will inspire, empower and entertain children, you can't go wrong with the Breges.
*Pat Slater, Head Librarian Children's Services Redford, MI.*

It was a happy day for us, made happier with your charm, talent, and great humor. Your creative team, Darrin, Karen and Mick won our hearts. We had lots of fun, and we learned so much about the craft. Delightful.
*Beatrice Catherino, Distinquished Emeritus, Department of English, Oakland Community College.*

Our students are still asking for your books in the library. I can't keep them on the shelves at all. You two were fabulous, engaging, exciting and fun. I will be sure to recommend you to every school I can think of.
*Shari Andrus, Media Specialist, Cedar View Elementary.*

We saw you at the Clinton-Macomb Library and became instant fans. Your message about reading and working hard and practicing is just what kids need! Your entusiasm is infectious! You guys are great!
*A Mom, Macomb Township, MI*

I hope you make some more new books. They were great! I would like to know you better!
*Elementary Student, Toledo, OH.*